THE TOWN MARSHAL

ROBERT VAUGHAN

WOLFPACK
PUBLISHING
— EST 2013 —

Published in the United States by Wolfpack Publishing, Las Vegas.

Wolfpack Publishing
6032 Wheat Penny Avenue
Las Vegas, NV 89122

wolfpackpublishing.com

Paperback ISBN: 978-1-64119-401-3
Ebook ISBN: 978-1-64119-400-6

Library of Congress Control Number: 2018958386

THE TOWN MARSHAL

CHAPTER 1

LINCOLN COUNTY, NEW MEXICO:

JOHN TUNSTALL'S BRITISH ACCENT, his knickerbockers and belted hunting jacket, made him stand out among all the residents of Lincoln County. He had come to America, and to the West, both out of a sense of adventure and for business opportunities. In the latter, he was doing very well. He had joined partnerships with Alexander McSween, a much-respected attorney, and with John Chisum, the largest cattleman in the area.

McSween and Tunstall had opened a mercantile house and recognizing the need for a bank, they opened one to be housed in the back of their store. In addition, they had begun to invest in cattle and had holdings on the Rio Feliz.

Their business successes were bound to make enemies and the men had made more than their share. When Tunstall, in his position as vice president of the bank, refused to honor a check for the struggling J. Dolan and

Company, a competing mercantile, he made an enemy of James Dolan.

Now, on one February afternoon, a very angry Dolan had braced Tunstall in the street in front of the mercantile.

"Pull your gun, you mangy son of a bitch!" Dolan called.

Dolan's challenge was issued loudly enough to get the attention of anyone who happened to be on the street at the time. Tunstall was a known pacifist who never carried a gun, and everyone wondered how this was going to turn out.

"My good man," Tunstall replied to Dolan's invitation, "surely by now you are aware that I never carry a gun."

"Then get yourself heeled, Mister, 'cause this ain't goin' to end 'til one of us is lyin' dead in the street. 'N I'll tell you right now, it won't be me."

"I have no intention of acquiring a pistol," Tunstall said, "so if you are going to shoot me, you will be shooting an unarmed man."

"I'm armed, Dolan. Why don't you draw against me?"

The man who spoke was James Cooper. He wasn't old in years, but he had the hard face and eagle eye of one who had matured in the school of life. He was clean-shaven, taller than average and wide of shoulder, with gun metal gray eyes, and brown hair.

"Thank you, Mr. Cooper," Tunstall said, "but I believe we can convince this gentleman that violence isn't necessary. Can't we, Mr. Dolan?"

Dolan looked at the young man who had stepped up to defend Tunstall. He was one of Tunstall's employees, and though he was passed off as a cowboy, Coop, as he was called, was actually one of Tunstall's bodyguards. Coop was known to be very good with a gun, as were the other two bodyguards: Henry Brown and William Henry McCarty, sometimes called Henry Atrim and sometimes called William Bonney. But he was best known as Billy the Kid.

"It's your call, Dolan," Cooper said. "You can either do what Mr. Tunstall says and walk away, or you can go for your gun and die."

The expression on Dolan's face when he had first braced Tunstall, had been one of anger and confidence. Now, he was licking his lips nervously, and there was a noticeable twitch in his cheek.

"What's it going to be, Dolan?" Cooper asked, his voice calm and conversational.

"I . . . I ain't got no bone to pick with you, Cooper. My quarrel's with Tunstall. He didn't have no right to not give me my money. That's wrong. If you're gonna have a bank, you cash people's checks."

"Mr. Dolan, I can't honor a check if there aren't sufficient funds available to cover it. What kind of business would that be?" Tunstall asked.

"Well, it was mean—that's all I've got to say." Dolan stood there for a moment, aware that he was the center of attention. Then he turned and headed for the saloon.

By the time Tunstall and Cooper returned to the Rio Feliz south of Lincoln, word had already reached the ranch of the showdown in town.

"You should have killed Dolan while you had the chance," Henry Brown said. "He's not going to stop, you know. He's goin' to keep on bothering Mr. Tunstall until someday it's gonna come to a head. Then there's no tellin' what could happen."

John Tunstall smiled and shook his head. "You know I want to avoid gunplay if it's at all possible."

"A noble thought," Brown said, "but sometimes it may not be possible."

"My dear Henry, I'm sure not even James Dolan would shoot an unarmed man." Tunstall turned and headed for the house.

"I wish I could be as sure of that as he is," Henry said. "Otherwise why does he think he needs bodyguards?"

Coop raised his eyebrows. "Where's The Kid?"

"Humph. You know where he is," Dick Brewer, the ranch foreman said as he approached the men.

"Over at Arino's place pining for his daughter?" Coop asked.

"That's where he is, all right," Brewer said.

"The Kid said he wanted to get in some shootin' practice later today," Brown said. "Coop, you should join us."

"Maybe later," Coop replied. "Mr. Tunstall said he wants to see me."

"All right, come on down when you can."

A few minutes later Coop knocked on the door of the library.

"Come on in, Mr. Cooper," Tunstall invited. He was ensconced in an oversized leather chair.

"You said you wanted to see me?"

"Yes, I want to thank you for coming to my defense today. And I appreciate that you kept your head and did not let the matter escalate," Tunstall said. "I have no doubt that Mr. Dolan knows of your proficiency with a gun."

"Yes, sir," Coop said. "I'm glad it didn't have to go any

further, but you have to understand that if it had, I would have been prepared to stop Dolan."

"Yes, and it was obvious that Mr. Dolan knew that as well. I do believe that it was your willingness to carry through, and his awareness of that determination, that prevented any actual shooting."

Coop felt uncomfortable as he listened to Mr. Tunstall's kind words. In his mind, he had been doing the job he was hired to do. Now he looked around the library. Three walls were covered with shelves filled with books.

"If you see something you like, feel free to take it to the bunkhouse with you."

"Thank you, Mr. Tunstall, but I'd rather not."

Tunstall chuckled. "I understand. You're different from the others, Coop. You have an appreciation for the written word."

"Yes, sir," Cooper replied. "What are you reading?"

"It's *The American Senator*, a novel written by Anthony Trollope. You should read it; it will give you some insight into England."

"*The American Senator* is about England?"

"Yes, don't be misled by the title. It's a device Trollope uses to provide an outsider's perspective of England. I think you might enjoy it."

"Thank you, Mr. Tunstall, I shall look forward to reading it, some day."

"Both Mr. McSween and I have noticed that you aren't like the other cow hands. How much education do you have, Coop?"

Cooper looked around to see if anyone else was in the room. "I, uh, have two years of college, but I would just as soon none of the others know."

Tunstall chuckled. "Do you think the others don't know? Oh, they may not know the specifics, but I guarantee you, there isn't a man on this ranch who doesn't know that you are well educated. Where did you go to school?"

"University of Missouri."

"Why didn't you finish?"

"My father died and my mother remarried. I couldn't get along with the man she married, so I left before I did something I would live to regret."

Tunstall nodded his head. "Would you be interested in another position? Alex says Mr. Chisum is in need of a more competent bookkeeper, and we think you may be just the man to take on the job." The Alex, Tunstall was speaking of was Tunstall's partner, Alexander McSween.

Coop lowered his head. "I appreciate your confidence in me, but . . ."

"Is it true that you killed a man in Texas?"

Coop raised his head, startled by the question.

"It is true, isn't it?" Tunstall held out his hand. "This is no condemnation, Mr. Cooper. Knowing you as I do, I'm sure there was ample justification."

"I had no choice," Coop said. "It was in Tarrant County."

"Was he a Texas Ranger?"

Cooper nodded. "He came after me for something I didn't do. If he'd been willing to take me in, I would've taken my chances with a jury trial. But he made it clear the only way I was going in was belly down over a horse. He drew on me and I shot him."

"And now you are a wanted man."

"Jackson F. Copley is a wanted man, but as far as I know, James F. Cooper isn't."

"Would the F. by chance stand for Fenimore?" Tunstall asked.

Coop smiled. "It does now, though originally it was Frank. And now I guess my secret and my life are in your hands."

"Just as mine was in yours, earlier today," Tunstall said. "Worry not, Mr. Cooper. Your secret is safe with me. But now I want you to consider seriously the position I have offered you. I know you will do well. Let me know your decision, and I will pass it on to Mr. Chisum."

LATER THAT AFTERNOON COOP, Henry Brown, and Billy the Kid were shooting at three empty cans they had placed on a fence rail.

"When I count to three draw and shoot," Henry said. "One, two, three!"

All three men drew at the same time, but there was enough separation in the sound of the shots to determine who had shot first. It was obviously Henry. It was difficult to tell whether Coop or The Kid had fired next, but when it was over, Coop's can was still sitting on the fence rail.

"Damn, Coop," The Kid said with a little laugh, "I guess it's a good thing we wasn't in a gunfight. You would 'a been left suckin' hind tit."

"That's no problem," Coop said. "I'll just remember never to get into a gunfight with either one of you."

"We'd better set up our cans and try it again," Henry said, as he started toward the fence.

"My can's good right where it is," Coop said.

"Really?" Henry drew his pistol and fired. Coop's can flew off the fence rail.

"Hmm, it looks like you might have to go get it after all," Henry said with a little chuckle.

For the next half hour, as the three men took target practice, Coop stayed even with Henry and The Kid. By the time the cook started banging on the triangle for supper; all three cans had so many bullet holes in them that they barely held together.

"What do you say we go into town after we eat?" Henry suggested.

"What good do you get out of going to town?" The Kid asked. "You don't drink, you don't play cards; hell, you don't even cuss, and I know you ain't goin' to be messin' around with no woman. So why would you want to go into town, anyway?"

"Because somebody has to keep you two out of trouble," Henry said.

JAMES DOLAN WAS SITTING at a table in the Monsanto Saloon, staring morosely into his mug of beer.

"I should have killed the son of a bitch when I had the chance," he said.

"You didn't want to do that," Deputy Baker said. "I mean, not in front of the whole town. Hell if you'd a killed him, Sheriff Brady would've had to arrest you." Baker took a swallow of his beer and smiled. "Now if you was a goin' to kill him, wouldn't it be better if you didn't do it in Lincoln?"

Dolan smiled. "Don't think I ain't gonna kill him. You

can put your money on the table, I'll find the right place and the right time."

"Well, well, well, look who just came in," Baker said nodding toward the door.

James Cooper, Henry Brown, and William Bonney stepped into the saloon, then crossed over to the bar. Coop and The Kid ordered beer; Henry ordered a sarsaparilla.

Dolan left the table and walked over to the bar and stood near them.

"You two boys come along to be nursemaid to the sody pop drinker, did you?"

"Mr. Dolan, you do seem to have a burr under your saddle," Coop said.

"Yeah, I do," Dolan admitted, "and the burr is that no-count Englishman you're workin' for. If he warn't too damn yellow to wear a gun, I would'a killed him today."

"Like you wanted to kill me?"

"I didn't have no fight with you, Cooper. You horned into my business all on your own."

"I guess you could say that," Coop said. He pointed to the gun in Dolan's holster. "Is that the gun you were going to use to kill Mr. Tunstall?"

Dolan slapped his hand on his holster. "What if it is?"

"That's a fine looking piece." Coop held out his hand. "You mind if I take a look at it?"

"Are you crazy? No man hands over his gun for no reason."

"Well, here's my gun. You can hang onto it while I look at yours, if you'd like."

Coop pulled his own pistol and handed it to Dolan,

handle first. Dolan looked at it for a moment, then took the gun and smiled.

"You're in a hell of fix now, ain't you? My hand is full, and your holster's empty."

"I am if you say so, but I expect even you wouldn't shoot me in cold blood," Coop said, "especially with the sody pop drinker and his nursemaid standing here beside me."

"I don't know why you want to look at my gun, but go ahead," Dolan said as he removed his gun and handed it to Coop.

"I'll tell you why, Dolan. Earlier today you wanted to use this gun to kill me, and I'm not sure you have that out of your mind yet. I figure if I get a good feel of it, well, it might even the odds a bit if it ever did come to an actual fight between us."

Coop took Dolan's pistol, turned his back to Dolan and aimed toward one of the windows. He twirled the pistol around his finger, then held it in both hands for a closer examination. Finally he turned around and handed the gun to Dolan.

"Yes, sir, that's a mighty fine pistol you've got there," Coop said as he retrieved his own pistol and returned it to his holster.

With pistol in hand, Dolan called out a challenge to Coop.

"Draw!" He brought the pistol up pointing it toward Coop.

Coop smiled and lifted the beer to his lips just as Dolan pulled the trigger. The hammer fell on an empty chamber. He pulled the trigger again and again.

"What the hell?" he shouted in frustrated anger.

"Like I said, that's a mighty fine piece you have there. But even a pistol as fine as that one, won't shoot if you don't have any bullets."

Coop opened his other hand to show the bullets he had removed from Dolan's gun.

The other patrons of the saloon who had braced themselves for a gunfight, roared in laughter almost as much from a release of tension, as from the humor of the event.

CHAPTER 2

A FEW DAYS LATER COOP WAS GIVING HIS HORSE A RUB-
down when he saw Dolan and several men riding up to
the Rio Feliz ranch.

"Henry, we've got company coming," he called back
into the barn.

Henry stepped out of the barn and looked toward the
men. "I don't think Dolan's a comin' to have tea with the
boss," he said. "And ain't that the deputy he's got
with 'im?"."

The two stood there and watched as the riders passed
under the arch that marked the entrance to the ranch.

"Get Tunstall out here," Deputy Sheriff Matthews
ordered.

"What do you want him for?" Henry asked.

"This posse's here on official law business," Matthews
said, as he reined his horse to a stop in front of the two
men. "Now unless you want to go to jail for interferin'
with Sheriff Brady's order, you'll get that bastard out here
like I said."

Dick Brewer, foreman of the ranch and another cowboy came up to join Coop and Henry.

"What's goin' on here?" Brewer asked.

"Brewer, you get Tunstall out here right now, or we're goin' to start burnin' down some buildin's," Matthews called.

"Hell, why don't we just commence a killin' 'em now," Frank Baker said. "We all know it's a' goin' to come to that sooner or later."

"Baker, you'll be the first one to die," Coop said as he lowered his hand toward his holster.

"Shut up, Frank, I'm runnin' this here posse," Matthews said, holding his hand out.

At that moment Tunstall arrived, doing so without having to be fetched.

"Good morning, Deputy Matthews. From the number of men you have with you, I take it this isn't a social visit. May I inquire as to its purpose?"

"John Tunstall, I have a court order here that says I'm attaching this ranch and all the livestock," Matthews said.

"You're attaching my property? Why?"

"I just told you why. On account of I've got a order from a judge that's tellin' me to do it," Matthews replied as if that were reason enough.

"One's property cannot be attached without reason. I am not in debt to the bank, nor do I owe anyone. I don't know what gives you the right to levy an attachment."

"I don't know the reason," Matthews replied. "All I know is I was given this attachment to serve 'n here it is."

"Deputy, you said the ranch and the livestock. Until this all gets straightened out, can we leave the cattle in place?" Dick Brewer asked. He took in the posse with a wave of his hand. "I doubt that more than two or three of these men have ever driven cattle, and yes, it's only twenty miles into town, but the first ten miles of any drive are always the hardest. Besides, once you get 'em to town, where're you gonna keep 'em?"

"Don't listen to 'im," Dolan said riding up beside the deputy. "You leave them cows here they'll just run off with 'em."

"Have you ever drove cattle, Dolan?" Matthews asked. "I have, 'n it ain't no easy job. Besides which, I wasn't told to *take* no cattle, I was just told to serve the attachment 'n that's what I just done."

Matthews stood in his stirrups and looked around at the house, bunkhouse, barn and corral.

"All right," he said as he sat back in his saddle. "I don't see no reason why I can't leave the cattle here. We'll be goin' back to town now. Don't you go tryin' to sell nothin' now, on account of as long as you got ever' thing attached like you have, you ain't actual got nothin' you can sell."

"Hey, Matthews," Henry said. "What makes you think you're going to get out of here alive?"

"What?" Matthews replied, gasping in surprise at the question.

"Look around you and tell me what you see."

By now there were more cowboys gathered than there were members of the posse, and all of them were armed.

"Now hold on, I don't want no trouble here!" Matthews said, his voice strained. "I mean all I come out here to do was serve this attachment. I didn't come out for no war."

"It looks like you've got one," Henry said.

Tunstall held out his hand. "Gentleman, I appreciate

the support, but I prefer to have this end without violence. Deputy Matthews, you have done your job; please go now, and leave us in peace."

"We'll do that." He jerked his horse around and headed down the lane. The others followed, though it was obvious that Dolan and Baker were unhappy about it.

Tunstall and his men watched the posse ride away, then he nodded at his foreman as he started toward the house.

"Okay, men, this don't change nothin'. We still got work to do," Brewer said to the others.

Everyone returned to their tasks, but a few minutes later Chico Arinas, the man Tunstall was calling his butler, came to Coop.

"Senor Coop, *el jefe* wishes you to come to The Big House."

"The boss wants to see me, does he? All right."

Coop let the horse loose in the corral, then walked up to The Big House. The house was, as the name implied, quite large: two stories with a porch that spread all the way across the front. It was white, except for the green shutters and door.

Mr. Tunstall, as Coop knew he would be, was in the library.

"If this is about the job you offered me, I think I'd rather stay where I am," Coop said as he stepped into the library.

"I thought that would be your answer, but this is something else." He was looking over the bill of attachment which the deputy had served. "I want a second pair of eyes to look at this. It says that I owe Dolan and Company a good deal of money, which on the face of it is ridiculous. Why would I run up a big bill at a competitor's store? Yes, I've used credit with them when I have to, just as everyone else does, but I've always paid the bill promptly. This thing looks like it's for everything I've charged since I've been in Lincoln, and quite frankly, it's more than I can pay right now," Tunstall said. "And, to make matters worse, the way I read this paper, I can't sell any of the cattle to pay the bill even if it was real. That restriction just about guarantees that I won't be able to meet the payroll by the end of the month."

"Whether you can pay or not most of the men will stay with you. You know Dick Brewer will stay, as will Henry, The Kid, and I."

"I sincerely appreciate that," Tunstall said, "but I may have found a loophole in this warrant. I want you to read it, and if you see what I see, then I'll be convinced that it's an option that may resolve my dilemma."

"All right," Coop agreed.

Coop began reading, and the more he read, the angrier he got. The attachment said Tunstall owed J. Dolan and Company for "goods that had been bought on credit." The amount supposedly owed, was considerably less than the value of the ranch at the Rio Feliz, even if none of the livestock had been included. But the warrant specifically included all the cattle, and it also stated that no money could be borrowed against the ranch in order to satisfy the lien.

"This is unbelievable," Coop mumbled as he continued to read. Then he stopped and looked up.

"The horses!"

"You see it too," Tunstall said, a smile crossing his face.

"I can't find horses mentioned anywhere in this lien,"

Coop said as he reread the paper. "You could sell half a dozen of them, probably to the stage coach station right here in Lincoln, and that would give you enough money to satisfy this debt and free up your herd."

"That was my thinking," Tunstall said.

"It really makes me angry that you have to do this, though," Coop said. "If you don't owe the money this time, what's to keep Dolan from pulling this stunt again?"

"For one thing, when I pay this alleged debt, I'll insist that I get a receipt declaring full and complete payment. Then I'll never darken Dolan's door again, no matter how far we have to go to fill our needs."

"Yes, sir, that'll work," Coop said. "I just hate it that you'll be giving that son of a bitch money that isn't his."

"Right now, my friend, it seems it's the price of doing business."

A FEW DAYS later Tunstall along with Dick Brewer, Bob Widenman, John Middleton, and Billy the Kid set out for Lincoln with six horses. They left early in the morning and expected to cover the twenty miles by late afternoon.

Trailing at a considerable distance behind them was a wagon being driven by Henry Brown. Coop was riding on the seat beside him.

"A newspaper? Are you kidding me?" Henry asked.

"No, I'm serious. When I was in school I put out a newspaper. I wrote the stories and my friends and I would print them out by hand. In a couple of hours we'd have one for every kid in school."

"I'm glad I wasn't your friend then," Henry said. "You

wouldn't catch me sittin' there for two hours printin' out somebody else's words."

Coop elbowed Henry in the ribs. "Oh, yes, you would have done it."

Henry shook his head. "Not me. I can't hardly read my own writin' when I know what it's supposed to say so what makes you think I'd a done it for you?"

"Because I had a secret weapon," Coop said. "My sister, Emmaline, was always there, too. She was the prettiest girl in school, and every guy I knew wanted to be the one to take her to the box social."

"Why you old son of a gun, using your sister like that. Did she know what you were doing?"

"Are you kidding? I think she got a kick out of it."

ABOUT A HALF-A-MILE ahead of the wagon, Tunstall and the others were moving the horses at a good pace when they heard a sound coming from a nearby thicket.

"Hey!" Brewer said. "Did you hear that? That was a turkey! What do you say, Mr. Tunstall? Can me 'n Widenmann go get us a couple? They'd sure make good eatin' for supper."

"Go ahead," Tunstall replied. "I rather like the taste of wild fowl."

"You want to come too, Kid?"

"No, I'll stay with Mr. Tunstall."

"All right. Come on, Bob, let's get us a turkey," Brewer said.

With Brewer and Widenmann gone, that left only The Kid and John Middleton with Tunstall. The Kid saw them first.

"Mr. Tunstall, look up ahead of us," The Kid said. "There must be twenty or thirty riders comin' toward us."

"I wonder what they want," Middleton said.

"I don't know, but it doesn't look good," The Kid said.

"Maybe we should drop back to the wagon," Tunstall suggested. "Let the horses run."

"Yeah, if it amounts to somethin', I want Coop and Henry's guns with us," The Kid said. "Come on, let's gallop!"

The Kid and Middleton turned to gallop the half mile back to the wagon, certain that Tunstall was with them.

But he wasn't.

Tunstall, believing that reason could prevail, started on a trot to meet the approaching riders.

Before Tunstall could speak, Billy Morton took aim and shot him. Then a man named Jesse Evans rode up and fired a bullet into Tunstall's head, killing him instantly.

"Let's kill his damn horse too," Morton said, and several of the riders shot the horse.

"What the hell was that?" Henry asked.

"Gunfire," Coop said ominously. "Must be trouble."

At that moment The Kid and Middleton came galloping toward them.

"What happened?" Henry asked.

"About thirty men came down on us," The Kid said. "We had to skedaddle."

"Where're the others?" Coop asked.

"Brewer and Widenmann rode off to hunt for turkeys, but even if they'd been there, we still couldn't have held 'em off," Middleton said. "That's why we had to run."

"But where's Tunstall?" Coop asked.

"He's right . . . ," The Kid said, as he turned in his saddle. "Mr. Tunstall?"

The Kid's call was unanswered.

"Damn," Henry said. "You didn't leave him with thirty men comin' at 'im?"

"I swear, fellas, we all took off together and I thought he was right behind us!" The Kid said.

"I'm goin' up to check on 'im," Henry said, snapping the reins against the back of the team. "Coop, you can hop down if you don't want to come with me."

"I'm going with you, partner," Coop said. There was a rifle lying in the foot-well of the wagon and Coop picked it up, then jacked a round into the chamber.

"By damn I'm comin' too," The Kid said, and with the team pulling the wagon at a trot, and the two riders keeping pace, they hurried to close the distance between them and the spot where The Kid and Middleton had encountered the posse.

Coop may not have been the first to see him, but he was the first to comment. "Oh, Lord," he said. "Look at that."

It took almost a full minute until they reached the gory scene. Both John Henry Tunstall and Derbyshire, his black thoroughbred horse, were lying in the road. Blowflies were already buzzing around them, indifferent to whether their host was horse or human.

Coop jumped down from the wagon before it was stopped and ran to the body. He saw the bullet hole in Tunstall's forehead, and for a moment Coop fought back nausea. In some sort of bizarre display, the horse's head had been placed on Tunstall's hat.

"What the hell happened here?" Brewer asked, arriving on the scene.

Widenmann, clutching a dead turkey by its legs, was right behind Brewer.

"They got him," Coop said as he rose from the body. "A shot in the head."

"Damn it, damn it, damn it," The Kid as he pounded a fist into the palm of his hand. "I swear I'll kill every one of the sons of a bitches who had anything to do with this. John Tunstall was the only man who ever gave a damn about me, and I won't forget it."

"I'll be right beside you, Kid," Henry said.

Coop nodded his head in agreement.

CHAPTER 3

THE NEXT DAY A CORONER'S JURY NAMED FRANK BAKER, Billy Morton, Tom Hill, Jesse Evans, Gorge Hindman, and Coop's nemesis, James Dolan, as those responsible for the death of John Henry Tunstall. In addition they added, "others not identified," for reports were that there had been at least two dozen men in the posse that intercepted Tunstall on his way into town.

Upon learning the findings of the coroner's jury, Justice of the Peace John B. Wilson issued warrants for the arrest of the accused men.

"What are you going to do about this, Antanacio?" Dick Brewer asked Lincoln Constable Antanacio Martinez.

"What can I do? I am but a city constable; I don't even have one deputy."

"I'll be a deputy," Billy the Kid said.

"So will I," Coop added.

"And I'll be the third one," Henry said.

"All right," Martinez said. "Hold up your right hands, but I don't have any badges for you."

"That won't matter," The Kid said. "Everybody will know soon enough that we're deputies."

After the constable left, the three were standing in front of his office.

"Now what?" Coop asked. "Where do we start?"

"More than likely there'll be talk at Monsanto's," Henry said. "Let's go there first and see what happens."

MONSANTO'S SALOON was next door to the court house. The saloon was filled with customers and a couple of percentage girls were moving among the tables flirting with the men to get them to buy drinks. An older, bald-headed man was at the back of the room playing the piano, though the music could barely be heard over the sound of dozens of spirited conversations.

"Look at 'em," The Kid said. "There ain't no doubt in my mind—some of these men were in the posse that killed Mr. Tunstall."

Henry pulled his pistol, pointed it up toward the ceiling and fired. The loud bang of the gunshot brought all conversation to a halt and shocked the piano player as he jerked his hands away from the keys. Everyone in the room: customers, bar-girls, piano player, bartender, and janitor looked toward the three men, one of whom was holding a smoking gun.

"We've just been deputized!" Henry called out to them. "We're lookin' for Frank Baker, Billy Morton, Tom Hill, Jesse Evans, Gorge Hindman, and that son of a bitch, James Dolan. They're all wanted for the murder of John Tunstall."

"And there ain't no doubt in none of our minds but

what there warn't a lot of you in that posse too," The Kid added. "And if you was one of 'em, you'd best get on out of the county, plumb out of New Mexico even, 'cause when I find out which ones of you was in that posse, I aim to kill you."

"Drop that gun, Brown!" The loud, authoritative voice belonged to Sheriff Brady.

"He's got a gun stickin' in my back," Henry said as he dropped his gun.

"You other two shuck outta them gunbelts," Brady added, looking toward Coop and The Kid.

"Sheriff, I think you're making a mistake here," Coop said. "We've been deputized by Constable Martinez to go after the men who killed John Tunstall, and we're just doing our job."

"No, what you're doing here, is disturbing the peace. Now, come along with me. You boys are going to jail."

As the jail was just across the street from the saloon, Brady didn't have far to take them.

"Sheriff, you are exceeding your authority here," Coop said as the three men were put into the single cell. "We're deputies, duly commissioned by Constable Martinez, and on authority of a warrant issued by the coroners' jury and Judge Wilson."

"You fired a pistol in a public building," Sheriff Brady said turning to Henry. "That's disturbin' the peace."

"But we didn't do anything," The Kid said.

Less than an hour after their incarceration, the three were ordered released by Judge Wilson.

THREE DAYS LATER A BUCKBOARD, carrying the polished

walnut coffin of John Tunstall, was brought into Lincoln. Every cowboy from the Rio Feliz Ranch, led by Tunstall's foreman, Dick Brewer, rode in a solemn column of twos behind the coffin. Cowboys from John Chisum's Bosque Grande outfit were behind the Rio Feliz riders. All the cowboys were dressed in their finest clothes.

Nearly all of Lincoln's 800 residents were turned out to watch the grim parade down Main Street. The cortege stopped in front of Tunstall's store, and the first six cowboys in the group, Brewer, Coop, Henry, The Kid, Widenmann, and Middleton, removed the coffin from the buckboard and carried it to the grave that had already been dug beside the Englishman's store.

"We ain't got no preacher in town," Brewer said. "So, I'm just goin' to ask a few of the boys to say a word or two. Coop, you're most likely the best one of us for words, why don't you go first?"

Coop looked around at those who were gathered for the funeral—at least thirty cowboys from the two ranches, then beyond them, citizens of the town. Some of those here, he was sure, had a part in the death of this fine man, but he had no idea who they were. He cleared his throat before he began to speak.

"John Henry Tunstall was a man of class, and grace. He was also a man of peace. He was unarmed when he approached a group of men to reason with them, and while in that vulnerable state, he was killed in an act of cold blooded murder. We, his employees and his friends, are here to honor the life of a good man, and to condemn the cowards who shot him."

As Coop turned away, Billy the Kid spoke up. "Mr. Brewer, I want to say something too."

"All right, Kid, you may speak."

The Kid looked out over those who had gathered for the funeral. He looked past the cowboys who represented the Tunstall and Chisum ranches, and at a group of men that he knew had shown some hostility to Tunstall during his life.

"We've got warrants which gives us the authority to go after Baker, Morton, Hill, Evans, Hindman, and Dolan, and believe me we'll find 'em. But I know they wasn't the only ones in that group of cowards that killed Mr. Tunstall. I know that some of you was there too, 'n I'm tellin' you here 'n now." The Kid pointed at the crowd. "I'm goin' to kill ever' damn one of you sons of bitches."

The Kid turned and walked away.

"I think it might be best now, if we just sort of bowed our heads in quiet while John's coffin is lowered," Alexander McSween said. His wife, Susan, was by his side.

After the funeral there was an uneasy truce in the town as those who had worked for Tunstall, and the men whose allegiance was to Sheriff Brady, and by extension, James Dolan, kept their distance from each other. A photographer, who had come from Roswell to take pictures of the funeral, began taking pictures of anyone who would pay him.

"Come on," The Kid said to the others. "Let's get our picture took."

"Why?" Henry asked.

"Why? Why, it'll make us famous, that's why," The Kid said. "Once you get your picture took, it'll be here long after you're gone."

"You go ahead," Henry said. "I've got no need to be famous."

"We'll hold your rifle," Coop offered.

"No, hell no," The Kid said, pulling his rifle closer to him. "I want my picture took of me holdin' on to my rifle."

"What about your hat?" Henry asked.

"I'm goin' to wear it too," The Kid replied touching the big sombrero he usually wore.

The photographer staged the picture in an arched alcove. The Kid held his rifle, a Winchester .44-40 with his right hand grasping it at the muzzle of the barrel. His left hand, with the fingers slightly curled, hung just below the holster as if in position for a fast draw. The hat was slightly cocked to the right, and his mouth was partly open.

"Close your mouth, why don't you?" Henry said.

"You're s'posed to smile when you get your picture took," The Kid said.

Coop laughed. "You call that a smile?"

"Gentlemen, please, be still while I take the picture," the photographer said. "Look at the birdie, the birdie so small, look at the birdie and don't move at all." There was flash of magnesium as the lens was tripped.

"Is that it?" The Kid asked.

"That's it," the photographer said. "I'll have the print ready for you tomorrow."

THE NEXT MORNING some of the Rio Feliz cowboys were gathered in the bunkhouse.

"I mean with Mr. Tunstall dead, we ain't really got no jobs now, do we?" Charlie Bowdrie asked.

"I don't know," Jim French said. "Until we hear from

McSween I reckon we're still employed. And Mr. Brewer'll still be in charge. I expect he'll tell us what to do."

"Yeah, well I'll tell you what I'm goin' to do," Frank McNabb said. "I plan to eat breakfast. At least the cook's still got a job, 'cause I can smell the bacon cookin'."

Coop had listened to the others without joining the discussion. He, too, was concerned as to what lay before them, and like the others, he missed Tunstall. The ranch owner had been more than his employer; Tunstall had been his friend. Of course, one of the things that made Tunstall so well liked by the cowboys, was that he was a friend to all of them, and in each case he managed to find a connection that was unique for that particular cowboy. With Coop it was a shared love of books plus Tunstall had encouraged him to pursue his dream of writing. Now, Coop would have no one to talk to about that ambition. He had suggested to Henry once that he wanted to start a newspaper, but Henry had not offered any support.

When the others filed out of the bunkhouse to go to breakfast, Coop followed behind them.

"Will you be staying, or leaving?" Henry asked as he fell in beside him.

"That's a good question," Coop said. "I really don't know what I'm going to do. If there's something here to stay for, I guess I'll stay. Because to be honest, if I have to leave, I don't have any idea where I'll go. I can't go back to Texas, and I won't go back to Missouri."

Henry laughed. "Me 'n you's in the same boat," Henry said. "Like you, things is just a little too hot for me back in Texas. 'N I sure as hell don't have any ambition to go back and settle in Rolla, Missouri."

"I suppose the only thing we can do now is wait and

see what's going to happen," Coop said. "I expect the Rio Feliz will be taken over by Chisum, unless McSween wants to keep it."

"What about Tunstall's family back in England? We know they've got money. Maybe one of them will come take over the place," Henry said.

"Maybe, but like I said, all we can do now is wait and see what happens."

THE COOK HAD PREPARED A PARTICULARLY good breakfast, perhaps because he realized that all the men needed a lift. He made bacon and hotcakes which everyone ate with relish. Then, just as breakfast was finished, Brewer stood up and called for everyone's attention.

"Men, I know you are wondering what's going to happen next. So I'll fill you in as best I can.

"Some of you may know that Mr. Tunstall had family back in England. It ain't likely that they're goin' to want to come over 'n run the ranch, so Mr. Chisum is goin' to buy it out 'n continue to run it, which means he'll be keepin' ever' one on so's we'll all still have our jobs."

There were several assertions from the men showing that they were pleased with the prospect.

"But, in addition to that, I've got another proposal." Brewer paused for a moment and let his eyes shift around the dining hall, falling on the face of every man present. "I've been appointed a senior deputy by Judge Wilson, and he tells me that makes my authority equal to that of Sheriff Brady. I'm gonna put together a group of deputies that I'm callin' the Regulators. And the purpose of the Regulators will be to find the named bastards that murdered Mr. Tunstall."

"What about Coop 'n The Kid 'n me?" Henry asked. "We was already deputized by Martiniz."

Brewer smiled. "You three will be my first deputies."

"Mr. Brewer, that's all well 'n good 'n ever'thing," The Kid said. "'N I sure as hell want all them men named by Judge Wilson, but I seen the ones that were comin' after Mr. Tunstall, 'n they was a hell of a lot more than just them six men. Mr. Tunstall was the first man that ever treated me decent, 'n I aim to make 'em all pay."

"Kid, I didn't say those six were the *only* ones we were goin' after," Brewer said, "but seein' as how we know their names, it seems only fittin' that they'll be the first ones we go after.

"Now, I'm goin' to need some volunteers for the Regulators."

Every man present raised his hand.

Brewer nodded his head. "I thought this would be how it is, but some of you are goin' to have to stay behind 'n run the ranch so the rest of us will have a job to come back to. So I'll pick out the ones that'll be ridin' with me."

In addition to Coop, Henry, and The Kid, Brewer chose Charlie Bowdre, Jim French, William McCloskey, Frank McNab, John Middleton, J.G.Scurlock, Sam Smith, and Mo Turley.

"All right," he said, "from now on, you boys will be members of the Regulators."

"Is this here a payin' job?" Turley asked.

"It is," Brewer replied. "Forty and found, just like you've been drawin' all along."

Turley shook his head. "If it's all the same to you, Mr.

Brewer, I'd just as soon stay here 'n work the ranch. Forty and found is good money for cowboyin', but it ain't enough for me to maybe get myself kilt."

"Mr. Brewer, I'd be proud to take his place," Fred Waite said.

"All right. Mo, you'll stay here and work the ranch. Fred, we'll be proud to have you with us."

"There ain't no hard feelin's or nothin' from you other boys, is there?" Mo Turley asked.

"No hard feelings from me, Turley," Coop said. "It's as Mr. Brewer said—somebody has to keep the ranch going."

"Thanks," Turley said.

"Mr. Brewer, shouldn't we be sworn in or somethin'?" Henry asked.

"Good point," Brewer said. "All of you hold up your right hands."

The newly selected members of the Regulators did so.

"Do you swear to do what I tell you to do?"

"Hell, we been doin' what you tell us to do for more 'n a year now, I don't see as how this would be any different," Bowdrie said. The others laughed.

"You can put your hands down now. You're swore in," Brewer said.

CHAPTER 4

SOON AFTER THE FORMATION OF THE REGULATORS, A LONE cowboy came onto the Rio Feliz ranch.

"Hey, ain't that Mark Worley?" The Kid asked. "Don't he ride for Chisum?"

"I believe he does," Coop replied.

"I wonder what he wants," Henry asked.

"I expect we're about to find out."

"Is Brewer around?" Worley asked when he reached the three men.

"He's having a second cup of coffee," Coop said. "Come on, I'll take you to him. I expect you could use a cup yourself."

"Thanks. I left the Bosque Grande before sunrise."

Worley dismounted, and Henry led his horse over for water as Coop took the Chisum rider into the chow hall.

Dick Brewer was sitting alone at one of the tables and he looked up when Coop and Worley came in.

"You ride for the South Spring brand don't you?" Brewer offered Worley his hand. "What brings you out so early?"

"Mr. Chisum thought you'd want to know some of the men you're looking for are camped out on the Pecos," Worley said. "It's not far from the South Spring."

Brewer finished the coffee in one gulp then stood up. "Coop, tell the men to saddle up. We're goin' hunting."

"Yes, sir!" Coop said with a broad smile.

BEFORE NOON the Regulators spotted two men riding near the river.

"That's Billy Morton!" Billy the Kid said. "They say he's been braggin' it was his bullet that kilt Mr. Tunstall."

The Kid raised his pistol.

"Don't shoot! We're too far away," Brewer cautioned, but The Kid wasn't to be denied, and he fired at the two men.

As Brewer had warned, they were out of pistol range, and The Kid's shot served only to warn them of the Regulators' presence.

The Kid had worked with both Billy Morton and Frank Baker before he had joined the crew at the Rio Feliz, and he didn't have much use for either man. Baker was now Sheriff Brady's deputy, and upon hearing the gunshot, he and Morton urged their horses into a gallop. The Regulators went into pursuit.

Baker and Morton were firing at the men who were chasing them. They were on horseback and the distance was too great for any accuracy. The shooting did nothing but startle a few birds into flight.

Coop had never ridden so far, so fast, and he wondered how much longer the horses could hold up, not only his horse, but Morton and Baker's mounts as well.

The thought had barely passed his mind when he saw Baker's horse collapse in exhaustion. Morton's went down immediately after. The two men scrambled to get into a conveniently located prairie sinkhole.

"Dismount!" Brewer called. "Every third man hold the horses. The rest of you with me."

Coop drew the duty of holding his, Henry, and The Kid's horses, and he could hear them breathing heavily. He patted all three horses on their forehead, marveling that they had stood up to the long chase, while Baker and Morton's horses had collapsed.

There was some shooting from the advancing Regulators, but no shooting came back from the defenders.

"We give up! We give up!" Baker shouted from the sink hole. He held up a white handkerchief and waved it back and forth.

"Hold your fire men, don't shoot!" Brewer ordered. "Baker, you 'n Morton throw your guns over, then come out with your hands up."

Coop saw two guns tossed out of the hole; then because the shooting was over, he started forward, leading the horses.

"You're our prisoners now," Brewer said.

"What . . . what are you going to do with us?" Baker asked.

"I'm not real sure," Brewer said. "To tell you the truth, I'm sorry you gave up. I wish you two had been man enough to fight it out 'till the end."

"Hell, let me just kill the sons of bitches now," The Kid said. "They sure ain't fit to live."

"You can't let him do that," Baker said. "You got to

protect us, Brewer. I'm a deputy and I know that's how it's supposed to be."

"We'll get you some horses; then we'll ride back to Lincoln," Brewer said.

"What good's that goin' to do us?" Henry asked. "If we turn 'em over to Sheriff Brady, he'll just let 'em go. It's like Baker said, he's Brady's deputy, 'n him 'n Brady is good friends."

"Then we'll turn 'em over to Martinez."

"And what's the city constable gonna do with 'em?" The Kid asked. "I know—he's gonna put 'em in Brady's jail, and then what in hell is Brady gonna do with his friends?" The Kid shook his head. "No way is these two gonna be turned over to Brady if I have anything to say about it."

"We'll cross that bridge when we come to it," Brewer said, "but right now we got to get 'em some horses. In the meantime, you two start walkin'."

"WE SHOULD'A BROUGHT SOMETHIN' we could tie 'em up with," Brewer said when he dismounted at Chisum's South Spring Ranch. "McCloskey, keep 'em covered while we arrange for horses. If anybody thinks he needs to get a fresh mount before we start for Lincoln, now's the time to do it."

"All right," McCloskey agreed and drawing his pistol he held it level toward Baker and Morton.

"You ain't plannin' on hangin' us when you get us to town, are you?" Baker asked. "'Cause if you are, you gotta know that Sheriff Brady ain't goin' to let that happen."

"It was legal what we done when we shot Tunstall,"

Morton said. "He was movin' them horses, 'n they wasn't supposed to go nowhere."

"Hey, McCloskey, them boys givin' you any trouble?" The Kid asked as he and Coop came walking back, leading fresh horses. Coop was leading two horses, one for himself and one for McCloskey.

"Oh, they're just sayin' as how they had a right to shoot Mr. Tunstall," McCloskey said, turning his head toward Henry.

"Here's a couple of mounts for you two," Henry said, as he approached the prisoners.

Morton got on the horse, but McCloskey was standing too close with his drawn gun. Morton kicked McCloskey, and then Baker grabbed the gun. He shot McCloskey at close range.

"Uhn!" McCloskey grunted, slapping his hand over the bleeding bullet hole in his stomach as he fell to the ground.

"Shoot as many as you can!" Morton shouted, as Baker turned the pistol toward Coop.

Both of Coop's hands were occupied, holding onto the reins of the horses, but even if his hands had been empty, he wouldn't have been able to pull his gun in time. Baker had the pistol in hand and was coming back on the hammer.

With a sense of resignation, Coop felt he was about to die. He heard the roar of a pistol shot but to his surprise, he wasn't the one shot. Instead he saw Baker going down with a look of shock on his face.

During the excitement, Morton had mounted one of the horses and kicking its sides, he raced away. The others mounted quickly and gave chase.

"Coop, see to McCloskey!" Brewer ordered, as approached the scene.

Coop knelt beside McCloskey and saw that his eyes were open, but unseeing. He put his finger on McCloskey's neck. He felt nothing, and McCloskey wasn't breathing. "He's dead."

Coop had not gone with the others and now he heard a loud barrage of shots being fired. After a few minutes the others came back, laughing and talking loudly.

"How many times did we kill that son of a bitch?" McNab asked. "Ten, eleven times?"

"You can only kill a person once," Scurlock said.

"Yeah? Well we sure put enough bullets in 'im to kill 'im more 'n once. At least enough to make certain he was kilt."

Henry and The Kid came over to Coop, who was standing over Baker's body.

"You all right?" The Kid asked.

"Yeah," Coop replied with a sheepish grin. He nodded toward Henry Brown. "Thanks to Henry, I am."

"It was nothing," Henry replied.

"It may be nothing to you," Coop replied, "but it was my life, and I mean it when I say thanks to you. You saved my life, Henry."

"If we was Injuns, that would mean you belong to me now," Henry said. He laughed. "Too bad we ain't Injuns; it might be good to be able to boss you around."

"Me no belong to you, but me be good friend," Coop teased, talking as he thought an Indian might talk.

"What do we do now, Brewer?" Sam Smith asked.

"Get Morton and Baker thrown over these horses. We're goin' to take 'em into town 'n let ever' one of 'em see that we're serious about takin' care of the sons of bitches who killed Mr. Tunstall."

IT TOOK them just under four hours to get to town and though it wasn't yet dark, the sun was low and Main Street was in shadow. They entered town in a precise column of twos, as if they were a troop of cavalry. Brewer rode in front, and immediately behind him rode Coop and Henry, each of them leading a horse over which a body had been draped. Coop was leading Morton's horse, while Henry had Baker's.

A significant number of the town's people turned out to watch the macabre parade with the two dead bodies, and the men riding in perfect formation. Few of the onlookers spoke, and when they did speak it was in hushed whispers. The loudest sound was the hollow clomping of the horses' hoof beats, the sound echoing back from buildings that faced the street.

As they rode by J. Dolan and Company, Dolan stood out front, glaring at them. There were people standing on the upstairs balcony of the Wortley Hotel. Beyond Tunstall's store they could see the mound of fresh dirt covering the Englishman's grave. A few of the bargirls were in front of Monsanto's Saloon, watching with the same morbid interest as the rest of the town's people.

They stopped in front of the jail, but Brewer didn't have to summon Sheriff Brady as he was standing out front watching as they arrived.

"What's this?" the sheriff demanded.

"All right, boys, dump the bodies," Brewer ordered.

Coop and Henry dismounted, then untied the ropes

and pushed the bodies off. The horses reacted nervously and tried to step away from what had been their load.

"Here's your deputies, Brady," Brewer said. "I don't rightly know if Morton was your deputy or not, but he was with Baker when we found them."

"You kilt 'em, and you dare to bring 'em into town and dump 'em at my doorstep?" Brady asked, his voice seething with anger. "Mister, you're guilty of murder. I'll see that you all hang!"

"Not so fast," Brewer replied. "In the first place, I'm the chief deputy, and Judge Wilson issued a warrant for the arrest of these two men. And in the second place, it was my intention to bring both of them in for trial. I gave them my word for safe passage into town, but Baker grabbed a gun and killed William McCloskey. Then he turned the gun toward James Cooper and he would've killed him if Henry Brown hadn't been there to kill Baker.

"And that makes that killin' what you call justifiable homicide," Brewer concluded.

"That explains Deputy Baker but what about Deputy Morton?"

"Morton violated his trust and ran. He was shot in legitimate pursuit."

"Deputy Brewer is right, Sheriff," Judge Wilson said as he stepped out of the crowd that had gathered. "Both of these shootings were legal. You need to take care of the bodies, and let these men get on about their legitimate business."

Sheriff Brady stood in front of the jail for a moment longer, the expression on his face showing that he was fuming inside.

"Get out of my sight, all of you," he said with an angry wave of his arm.

Brewer rode out to the side so he could see the Regulators, still in formation.

"Boys!" he called. "I'll meet you in Monsanto's. The first drink is on the Rio Feliz!"

The offer was met with spontaneous cheers from the men.

CHAPTER 5

WITHIN DAYS AFTER THE REGULATORS HAD DELIVERED Morton and Baker's bodies to Sheriff Brady, a private coach bringing Territorial Governor Samuel B. Axtell arrived in Lincoln.

"Thanks for comin', Governor," Sheriff Brady said as he opened the door to the coach. "Things are getting out of hand here and it needs to be put right."

"As soon as I figure out what's going on, I plan to hold a hearing," Governor Axtell said. "I need to get the word out to all interested parties to meet in the courthouse."

"You can hold it right now, Governor. Anybody that's got an interest is here in town already," Brady said.

"That will be for me to decide," Axtell said. "I want to talk to the people who were sympathetic to John Tunstall as well, and I doubt they are in town."

Brady didn't answer. He turned his back to the governor and walked back to the jail.

"HE SAID HE'S GOIN' to hold a hearing," Martinez said,

having ridden out to the Rio Feliz Ranch to tell Brewer and the others of the governor's arrival. "And he wants all interested parties to be present for the hearing."

"Don't do it, Mr. Brewer. They're trying to trick us, as sure as my name is Henry Brown."

"You may be right," Brewer said. He stroked his chin as he thought about it. "Still, I wouldn't like for some decision to be made that went against us just because we weren't there to represent our side."

"Let me go," Coop offered.

"What do you mean, let you go?"

"I mean, let me attend the hearing as advocate for the Regulators," Coop said.

"You mean be our lawyer? You're not a lawyer? We should get McSween."

"As I understand it, this isn't a trial," Coop said. "It's only a conference to mediate the difference between the belligerent parties. That being the case, I can be your advocate and mediator even without being a member of the bar, but I'll arrange for McSween to be there as well."

"Let Coop go to the hearing, Dick," Henry suggested. "He's 'bout the smartest man I've ever seen, 'n for sure he's the smartest one of us."

"All right," Brewer agreed with a nod of his head. "You can go, Coop, but I don't feel good about it; I feel like I'm puttin' you in danger. You're prob'ly right though, if there's some kind of hearing goin' on, I think our side should be heard."

"I'll tell you what I'll do," Martinez said. "I'll go back into town and get the governor's personal guarantee that he'll grant Cooper safe passage for a hearing tomorrow."

Brewer smiled. "Yes, do that. It'll make me feel a lot better."

BEFORE NOON the next day Martinez arrived at the Rio Feliz with a piece of paper signed by the governor.

Know ye all men by these presence that I, Samuel B. Axtell, Governor by Federal Appointment over the Territory of New Mexico, grant a guarantee of safe entrance and egress from the town of Lincoln, New Mexico Territory, to one James Cooper. This pass is good for the continuation of the Governor's Hearing on the events of discord now taking place in Lincoln County.

"Lord, this is so high-falutin' that I don't even know what the hell it says," Martinez said.

Coop read the pass, chuckled, then folded it and put it in his shirt pocket.

"It says I'll be safe. Constable Marinez, I'm ready to go," he announced.

"Hey, Coop, if that son of a bitch changes his mind and decides not to honor that, I'll come in, personally, and get your ass out of jail," Henry said.

"You're a good friend, Henry."

Henry laughed. "Hell, it ain't that. It's that you belong to me now, 'n I don't intend to let nobody else take you down."

Coop laughed as well. "Whatever it takes, Henry, whatever it takes."

SHERIFF BRADY and his new deputy met Coop and Martinez at the east end of town.

"Sheriff, this man has safe passage from the governor," Martinez said.

"Don't worry none about it," Brady replied. "Deputy Hindman and I are here to see that Mr. Cooper gets to the courthouse is all. With the Governor in town, it'd be a shame if he didn't make it."

WHEN THEY REACHED the courthouse Coop saw James Dolan standing in front of the building alongside L.G. Murphy, who had been a bitter enemy of Tunstall's. The two men glared at Coop as he dismounted and started toward the courthouse, but neither of them said a word.

John Chisum was waiting inside and Coop was pleased to see a friendly face. He looked around for Alexander McSween, but he wasn't there.

The courtroom was full of citizens, both from the town and the neighboring ranches, each one curious to see how this situation was going to be resolved. Coop started to take a seat near the back, but Chisum reached out to stop him.

"No, no, your place is up here," Chisum said, escorting him to a table in front of the galley as if he were a lawyer.

"I thought McSween would be here," Coop said.

"He would have been here if he had known this was happening," Chisum said, "but he's in Fort Worth tryin' to settle Emil Fritz's estate. You know the kinfolks are saying Alex stole the insurance money."

"Well did he?" Coop asked, a smile crossing his face.

"Hell, no, he didn't," Chisum said. "Have you ever met the governor?" He pointed out the man sitting behind the bench.

The man Chisum had identified as the governor had a high forehead, snowy white hair, and a rather prominent nose protruding from a red-veined face.

"Can't say that I have," Coop said as he stopped at the table.

"Are you the lawyer representing Wilson's Posse?" the governor asked.

"No, sir. Uh, that is, yes, Your Honor. I am representing Judge Wilson's posse, but I'm not a lawyer."

"It's all right if you're not a lawyer, young man," Governor Axtell said, and then he smiled. "I'm not a judge."

Axtell made a few raps with the gavel.

"This hearing will come to order," he said. "A few words of instruction. Although this is a hearing, and not a trial, we will conduct it with all the decorum and dignity of a trial. There will be no outbursts from anyone who has not been recognized by the bench, and any violators of this order will be expelled from this chamber.

"Now, unlike a court trial, we do not have a prosecution and a defense. What we have are opposing parties, which I will identify as the posse of Sheriff William Brady, and the posse of Justice of the Peace, John Wilson. Sheriff Brady, you may speak first."

Brady stood up and pointed toward Coop. "This son of bitch and the ones he runs with, murdered my deputy, and my friends, Frank Baker and Bill Morton."

Governor Axtell rapped his gavel on the bench. "Sheriff, I believe I said this hearing was to be conducted with decorum and dignity. I won't tolerate swearing in the testimony."

"All right, I'm sorry. But back to the men who call themselves the Regulators . . ."

"The what?" Governor Axtell asked.

"Wilson's posse, Governor. They're callin' themselves the Regulators."

"If they are Wilson's posse that is how you will refer to them."

"Yes, sir. Well, it started when John Tunstall was served with a warrant which seized his ranch and all his livestock to satisfy a debt. Then we caught him, red-handed, trying to move some horses out, in violation of the warrant. I sent a posse out to stop him, and during that confrontation, he was killed.

"After that his cowboys and friends took it upon themselves to run down two of my men who had been legitimate members of my posse, and they shot and killed both of them."

"Mr. Cooper," the governor said, "do you dispute the allegations made by Sheriff Brady?"

"Governor, I dispute the way in which he presented his side," Coop replied. "Take the shooting of Mr. Tunstall. I read the bill of attachment. In the first place, the amount of the alleged debt, was considerably lower than the value of the ranch and stock, and thus did not justify the seizure of the entire ranch. And in the second place, the horses were not included in the bill of attachment, so it was Mr. Tunstall's intention to sell the horses and settle the debt. But when he attempted to talk to the posse, he was shot down in cold blood by Bill Morton."

"Who you killed," the governor said. "Or do you deny that?"

"It was the intention of the senior deputy to bring both

Morton and Baker in to Lincoln to stand trial for Tunstall's murder," Coop said. "But Baker grabbed the gun from William McCloskey, shot and killed him; then turned the gun on me."

"Baker shot you?"

"No, sir. Baker was killed before he could shoot me. He was killed by—" Coop paused in mid-sentence. He was about to say that Baker was killed by Henry Brown, but he thought better of it. "He was killed by one of the men of Wilson's posse. When Morton saw that, he ran, but he was killed in the chase for his recapture."

"He, like Baker, was killed by Wilson's posse?" the governor asked.

"Yes, sir, and Governor, I hasten to add that not only was the posse legally constituted, we also had warrants for the arrest of Billy Morton and Frank Baker."

"You may have had warrants to arrest Deputies Baker and Morton," Governor Axtell said, "but you did not have the authority to administer summary justice without benefit of a trial."

"That's just what I've been a' sayin', Governor!" Sheriff Brady said, standing and pointing toward Coop. "Just pronounce the sentence, 'n I'll see to it that this son of a bitch is hung this very afternoon!"

"You are out of order, sir!" Governor Axtell said, sharply. "Sit down!"

After the chagrinned sheriff took his seat, the governor turned his attention back to Coop.

"Mr. Cooper, I have given my assurance that you will have safe passage in and out of town for the purposes of this hearing, and it is my intention to honor that pledge. However, effective immediately, all Judge Wilson's deputies' commissions are withdrawn, as are the warrants. The group known as Wilson's posse is to be disbanded, and all of you who call yourselves the Regulators are to return to your normal pursuits of commerce. There will be no more activity with regard to the unfortunate shooting of John Tunstall. Do you understand this order, Mr. Cooper?"

"Yes, sir, I do."

"Very good. Please convey this information to the others who work with you. Tell them they are excused from any past transgressions, but any such armed events between the group known as Wilson's posse, or the Regulators, as may happen in the future will constitute a violation of this order. You will be arrested, and you will be prosecuted. Have I made myself clear?"

"Yes, sir," Coop said. He heard the low voiced reactions from the others in the room, and he saw a huge smile spread across James Dolan's face.

"My pronouncement having been made, this hearing is adjourned," Governor Axtell said with a concluding blow from his hammer.

"YOU KNOW WHAT THIS MEANS, don't you, Cooper?" Dolan asked a few minutes later when they were outside the courthouse. "It means that if your damned Regulators don't disband, you'll be acting against the law. And I'll see to it that Sheriff Baker raises the biggest posse this county's ever seen just to deal with the likes of you." Dolan laughed. "And when I say dealing with you, I'm not talking about bringing you in for any kind of trial. No, sir. I'm talking about . . . what is it the governor said?

Summary justice? Yeah, I'm talking about administering summary justice."

"You have misread the governor's finding," Coop said. "He ordered the Regulators to discontinue serving the warrants, but he said nothing that would authorize the sheriff to attack a compliant band of Regulators."

Dolan chuckled. "I'm not exactly sure what your big words mean, but I do know what kind of justice you'll get —the same kind of justice Morton and Baker got."

Coop didn't honor Dolan with an answer. He walked out to his horse, but John Chisum stopped him.

"Let me buy you a good dinner before you leave town," Chisum offered.

Coop was facing a long ride back so he accepted the offer.

"So, tell me," Chisum said a few minutes later over a meal of roast beef and mashed potatoes, "how do you think Brewer is going to take the governor's order?""

"I honestly don't know."

"Please tell him for me, if you would, that my offer still stands. I intend to buy Rio Feliz from Tunstall's estate and in the meantime I'll keep it going by paying the salaries of all of John's employees. Oh, I have also satisfied the debt that John was supposed to have owed at Dolan's store."

"Yes, sir, I'll tell Mr. Brewer that." Coop said.

OVER IN THE Dolan and Company store Dolan, Murphy, and Brady were lamenting the outcome of the hearing.

"The governor should have declared the whole bunch of 'em outlaws," Brady said. "He should have put a reward of at least five hundred dollars on the head of ever'one of 'em. Hell, with that much money at stake, we could round up a posse big enough to kill 'em all."

"I agree," Murphy said. "It would be good to clear 'em all out and be done with 'em."

"We can get rid of one of 'em right now," Dolan said. Dolan was standing in front of his store, looking across the street toward Lambert's Café which was next door to the Wortley Hotel.

"What do you mean?" Murphy asked.

"I just saw Cooper go into Lambert's. We could take care of him now."

"No, we can't. Not without violating the governor's order. He said that Cooper would have safe passage out of here," Murphy said.

Dolan smiled. "Yeah, but he didn't leave, did he? He stayed right here in town, 'n the way I look at it, that safe passage is good only if he's leaving town. Ain't that right, Sheriff?"

"Yeah," Sheriff Brady said. "Yeah, that's the way I see it."

"So, what do we do about it?" Murphy asked.

"Luke Tomlin," Brady said.

"What?"

"Luke Tomlin's been wantin' to take Baker's place as my deputy. I'll send him over to arrest Cooper."

"I don't think Cooper will let himself be arrested," Murphy said.

"You don't say." Brady smiled. "That means I've got just the man to handle it."

CHAPTER 6

C‍OOP HAD JUST FINISHED HIS LUNCH WITH C‍HISUM AND stood up to leave the table when he heard his name being shouted in a loud, angry voice.

"James Cooper, you're under arrest!"

There was something about the shout that frightened everyone else in the café as people scrambled to move to the sides of the room getting clear of any potential gunfire.

"Who are you?" Coop asked. His voice was calm and he showed no sign of nervousness.

"Luke Tomlin, 'n I'm the new deputy sheriff. That gives me the right to arrest you."

Coop shook his head. "I don't think so, Mr. Tomlin. The sheriff's authority doesn't override the governor's authority, and he's given me safe passage to go back to the ranch."

"So what you're sayin' is, you ain't goin' to let yourself be arrested?"

Coop could see that Tomlin was licking his lips and

breathing heavily as he was getting more and more agitated.

"Deputy Tomlin, why don't we just let this go?" Coop said. "You go back to Sheriff Brady and tell him you ran me out of town. I'll leave right now."

Without another word, Tomlin drew his pistol. As soon as he cleared leather he smiled, knowing that he had beaten Cooper to the draw.

Coop purposely waited until Tomlin had his gun in hand, because he didn't want any misunderstanding by any of the witnesses. Then, as Tomlin began to bring his gun to bear, Coop, in a draw that witnesses would later compare to a streak of lightning, drew his own gun and fired.

Tomlin fired too, but it was a reflexive action because he fired as Coop's bullet plunged into his chest. Tomlin's stray bullet poked a hole in the floor of the café.

Coop held the smoking gun in his hand for a moment longer, just to make certain that he faced no further danger, then he holstered his pistol.

"I never seen nothin' but his shoulder jump a bit," one of the witnesses said.

The door opened then and Sheriff Brady came in with a broad smile on his face. "So, Luke, you had to shoot 'im did . . ." He stopped in mid-sentence and the smile on his face was replaced by a look of shock.

"What happened here?" He demanded.

"Tomlin come in 'n drawed on Cooper, onliest it was Cooper that drawed the fastest," one of the witnesses said.

"How do you know it was Tomlin that drawed first? When somethin' like this happens, you can't never be none too sure."

"Oh, we're sure all right," Chisum said. "Your deputy had his gun in his hand and it was half way up before Coop even started his draw."

"I don't believe it," Brady said. "There ain't nobody that fast."

"Believe it, Sheriff," Lambert said. "We all seen it."

"Yeah, well, I know for a fact that Tomlin was puttin' Cooper under arrest. 'N if a sheriff or a deputy is tryin' to arrest someone, it don't make no matter who draws first. The prisoner is the one who's guilty."

"Sheriff, I have a safe passage from the governor. Now you can either honor that pass and let me ride out of here, or you can challenge it, and go for your gun. I must tell you though you would be ill-advised to do so, because should you try, you'll wind up dead on the floor along with your erstwhile deputy."

GEORGE COE HAD RIDDEN to the Rio Feliz to report to the Regulators what had happened in town.

"'I must tell you though you would be ill-advised to do so, because should you try, you'll wind up dead on the floor along with your erstwhile deputy'." Coe laughed out loud. "That's just what Coop said to the sheriff all right. Ain't he the damndest talkin' thing you ever seen?"

Coe, who had been in the café to witness not only the shooting of Tomlin, but the showdown with Brady, was a cowboy from a nearby ranch. In the past, he'd been arrested and pushed around by Brady, and he decided he had had enough. He came to join the Regulators, and to report on what he had seen.

"What do we do now?" Billy the Kid asked.

"Boys, if you're with me, I say it's time we brought this thing to a head. I think we should go in to Lincoln and maybe have us a drink," Dick Brewer said.

"What if the sheriff gets him an idea that he don't want us there?" Henry Brown asked.

"Yeah, what if he does get such an idea?" Brewer asked, a leering smile crossing his face.

"THE REGULATORS IS COMIN' into town," Jack Long said, as he ran into the sheriff's office.

"How do you know?"

"I seen 'em, 'bout half a mile outta town, they was. They'll be here in just a few more minutes."

"We'll be waiting for 'em," Brady said as he took a rifle down from the rack.

"HEY, COOP, SEEIN' as how I saved your life, it seems to me like maybe you'll be buyin' me my first drink," Henry said.

"How long are you going to ride that 'you saved my life' horse anyway?" Coop asked.

"For the rest of your life, I reckon."

Coop laughed. "Well, I suppose you do have something there. All right, your first sarsaparilla is on me."

"Ha! What do you think about that, Kid? Coop's goin' to buy my drink."

The Kid didn't respond. Instead he was studying the town as they rode in.

"There's somethin' that ain't right, here."

"What do you mean?" Henry asked.

"Look around. Do you see anyone on the street?"

"Damn, Henry, The Kid's right. This town's empty," Coop said. "Mr. Brewer?"

"Yeah, I see," Brewer said. "Boy's draw your guns and be ready. I don't have a good feelin' about . . ."

That was as far as Dick Brewer got before he was knocked off his horse with a bullet that hit him right in the center of his forehead. After that, several ambushers jumped out from their hiding places and opened fire. Coop, Henry, and The Kid were the first to shoot back and their fire was deadly effective. Sheriff Brady went down, followed almost immediately by George Hindman.

After seeing Brady go down, the rest of the ambusher ran, leaving Brady and Hindman lying where they fell.

"I'm going to get me one of them Winchesters," The Kid said.

"Me too," Fred Waite said as both men started running toward the bodies.

Just as The Kid rolled Brady's body over to snatch his rifle, Ed Matthews, one of the sheriff's posse members, opened fire from the cover of a house across the street. He grazed Waite.

Emboldened by Matthews' shot, Jack Long began shooting at the Regulators and he hit Jim French.

"Let's get out of here, boys!" Henry called. "We're in the open!"

The Regulators galloped out of town, finding refuge with Garrison McKnight, a rancher who was sympathetic to their cause. McKnight tended to the wound Waite had suffered, and determining that it was minor, he suggested that the Regulators stay at the ranch until Waite had recovered.

McKNIGHT'S ASSOCIATION with the Regulators wasn't widely known so he had freedom of movement. A week after the Regulators arrived at his ranch, dispirited over the loss of Dick Brewer, McKnight took the buckboard into town for supplies. When he came back later, groceries weren't the only thing he had with him. He also had a flyer listing the warrants issued by the Lincoln County Grand Jury.

THE UNITED STATES vs J.G. Scurlock, Charles Bowdre, Henry Brown, Henry Atrim (aka William Bonney, Billy the Kid) James Cooper, John Middleton, Stephen Stevens, John Scroggins, George Coe, and Fred Waite. These men are wanted for the murders of Sheriff William Brady, George Hindman, Frank Baker, and William Morton.

"DAMN!" The Kid said. "This says we've got the whole of the United States against us."

"What do we do now?" Henry asked.

"For now I'd say we don't go into town," Spurlock said. "And, some thin' else. I think we should leave Garrison's Ranch,"

"Who made you the leader?" Bowdre asked.

"Brewer's gone and somebody has to be in charge," Coop said. "And I sure don't want the job. Do you, Charlie?"

Bowdre smiled, self-consciously. "No, I don't reckon I do, but I've got an idea where we can go."

"Where?" Spurlock asked.

"San Patricio."

CHARLIE BOWDRE HAD a special reason for choosing San Patricio. His wife and her large family of sheepherders lived there. The Regulators' presence in town wasn't resented because many of the people remembered Tunstall and what he had done to help them. They took a special liking to their guests and allowed them the run of the town. Coop, Henry, The Kid and many of the others, kept a lookout from the various rooftops, some even sleeping on them.

"We can't stay here," John Middleton said after several weeks. "These people are feedin' us and givin' us comfort. And what are we a doin'? We're puttin' their lives in danger. That's what we're a' doin'."

"What do you suggest we do?" Henry asked.

"I think we need to ride right into Lincoln and bring this thing to a head."

"With Brewer and McCloskey gone, there are only ten of us remaining," Coop pointed out.

George Coe smiled. "There are a hell of a lot more just like me. All we have to do is put out the word and they'll join us."

"All right, George, you're in charge of recruitment," Charlie Bowdre said.

CHAPTER 7

THE RECRUITING WENT WELL. COWBOYS FROM ALL OVER Northeast New Mexico were anxious to get back at the merchants of Lincoln, especially James Dolan. They felt Dolan had taken advantage of them long enough. And now George Peppin, the new sheriff, had gathered what seemed like a small army to make up his posse.

It was Peppin's posse that made the recruiting easy, for nearly every cowboy who joined them had his own story to tell of the aggressive nature of the deputies.

NONE of the street lamps were lit on the night the Regulators chose to ride into Lincoln, and because even the saloons were closed, there was no ambient light. It was also the dark of the moon making it necessary for the men to navigate in total darkness.

"Can't see a damn thing," one of the men said.

"Yes, but think of it," Coop said. "If we can't see, that also means we can't be seen."

"We can be heard though," Henry said. "Be quiet."

The conversation quieted and only the soft plodding of the hoof beats announced their entry.

"Damn, it's spooky," someone said a moment later.

His comment was followed by a chorus of "Shhh."

"Let's split up and find cover where we can," The Kid suggested. "Coop, Henry, you two come with me."

"I think we need a few more than just the three of us," Henry said.

"All right, we'll take a half dozen more. For now, the rest of you make your way over to the stone tower," The Kid said.

The tower The Kid mentioned had been built a few years back. At the time it had been used as a lookout for Indians.

"It's dark as pitch in there," one of them complained. This was the same man who, earlier, had declared that it was 'spooky'.

"You want to light one of the street lamps 'n stand under it?" Henry asked.

"No, hell no, if we did that, we'd be a wide open target."

"Then don't complain."

Coop, Henry, The Kid, and the group that had split off to come with them headed for Alexander McSween's house.

"McSween, it's me, Billy," The Kid called as he knocked on the door. "I've got some folks with me."

The door opened just a crack, and a small strip of light appeared in the night.

"Billy?"

"Yeah, let us in."

The door opened fully, spilling a wide bar of light. "Hurry in," McSween said.

The Kid was the first one in, and he stood by the open door, hurrying the others in. When the last one was inside, McSween closed and barred the door.

Besides McSween, there were three other women and a child in the house: McSween's wife, Susan, his sister in law, Elizabeth Shield, Elizabeth's ten-year old daughter, Minnie, and Katherine Gates, the local school teacher.

"Alex, I'm frightened," Susan said. "It's come to this. There's going to be shooting, isn't there?"

"I won't lie to you, Susan, there probably will be," McSween said. "But you know the walls to this house are thick adobe, and I'm sure we'll be safe in here."

"Do you know where Sheriff Peppin is?" Henry asked.

"He's been expecting something to happen. For the last couple of days, he's been gathering his posse and now he's got men scattered all over town. But for the most part, I'd say they're holed up in Dolan's store," McSween answered.

"Well then we may as well get comfortable folks; we're going to be here for a while," The Kid said.

Coop looked around at all the faces, gauging their expressions. He saw determination and even excitement among the other Regulators, concern in the face of Alexander McSween, and fear in the faces of Susan McSween and Elizabeth Shield. The child seemed more confused than frightened, and oddly, the school teacher didn't seem to be the least concerned.

"Susan, you might make us some coffee," McSween suggested.

"I'll help," Elizabeth offered. Katherine and Minnie joined the other two, which left the men alone.

"I'm sorry the ladies have to be mixed up in this," Henry said.

McSween shook his head. "I tried to get them to leave, but Susan wouldn't go, and the others wouldn't leave without her."

"I think you're right about the walls. As thick as they are, we should be all right if we stay inside and away from the openings," Charley Bowdre said.

"I can't believe you said that," The Kid said. "Don't forget we came here to take of things, to avenge the death of John Tunstall, 'n we can't very well take care of things by staying cooped up in here no matter how safe it is."

Soon, the women returned with the coffee. The men were given china cups that had painted flowers on them. Coop thought it an odd juxtaposition, when he thought about their mission. Any one of these men would kill a man at the slightest provocation, and yet they lifted the delicate cups to their mouths and sipped the coffee. When they were finished, the women took the cups and returned to the back of the house.

The men took up positions near the windows even though it was still too dark to observe anything happening outside. No one thought of sleeping. There was a lot of area to cover.

The house was a single story, but shaped like the letter "U", with four rooms on each wing joined by a formal parlor and a plaza in the center. The back of the plaza looked out over the Rio Bonito. Ironically, the house had been built by the best stone mason in town, George

Peppin, the very man who was poised to riddle the house with bullets.

In more peaceful times the McSween house, because of its size, was the center of social activity. Susan aggrandized everything, even fabricating her heritage, saying she was part of a royal family. This house had the finest and best furnishing including carpets and draperies at every window, but her most prized possession was a piano—the only one in town.

All of this ostentation caused the townspeople to distrust Alex's business dealings saying he was stealing from them when he tried to collect past debts. He was in the process of settling an estate for the Fritz heirs at the time the piano had arrived, and everyone believed he had taken money from the heirs—heirs who were friends of James Dolan. All of this friction, along with McSween's partnership with John Tunstall, only served to foment the current feud between the Regulators and the townspeople.

"There's been no shooting yet," Susan said as she crawled over to the window where Alex had taken his position. "Perhaps there won't be any."

McSween took Susan's hand in his as she sat beside him. "No matter how much we don't want it, there will be shooting."

"I almost wish it would start," Susan said as she laid her head on her husband's shoulder. "Almost anything would be better than sitting here waiting—waiting for people we know to start trying to kill us."

"Just remember," McSween said, "we didn't start this fight. Think about poor John. To my knowledge, he never owned a gun, much less fired one in anger."

"Why did they have to kill him? What did he do to them?"

Alex cradled his wife in his arms. "Only God knows what causes people to act the way they do."

Coop watched the tender scene between husband and wife. He looked around and saw that a couple of the men had stretched out and were now sleeping peacefully. What would tomorrow bring?

Elizabeth Shield and her daughter Minnie were huddled in the corner, both asleep as well. Catherine Gates, the schoolmarm, had moved off into a corner by herself. She dressed and wore her hair as conservatively as possible, but Coop could see that she was actually quite an attractive woman.

To help combat her nervousness and help ride out the 'silence before the storm,' she was reading a book.

"*The Vicar of Bullhampton*," Coop said, noticing the title of the novel. He nodded. "It's an interesting story in which the author creates sympathy for a fallen woman. You've chosen a very good book to while away the time."

"You know this novel?" Katherine asked, surprised by the comment.

"Yes, I've read it and enjoyed it. I was introduced to Anthony Trollope by . . . " he was going to say Mr. Tunstall, but he chose to hold his tongue. "You might like *The American Senator* as well."

"Oh, I plan to. Have you read it?"

"No, I have not." Coop looked away as he visualized Mr. Tunstall in his library, ensconced on his leather chair. That was the last book he ever saw John reading.

"Are you an educated man, Mr. Cooper?"

"Some say that I am," Coop replied, not wanting to go any further.

"Then what are you doing with these . . . I don't know what to call them? They certainly aren't gentlemen."

"I call them my friends." Coop was annoyed by the school teacher's insinuations about people she didn't know. "I can say that one man, Henry Brown, is my best friend. I couldn't abandon him now."

"Well, loyalty is quite commendable," Katherine said, realizing that she may have offended Coop.

"I won't bother you any more, ma'am. You go ahead and enjoy your book, while you can."

"Yes," Katherine replied. "While I can."

COOP DOZED off during the night, but was startled awake by the sound of gunfire. When he opened his eyes he saw morning light streaming in through the window where The Kid was standing. It was his shooting that had awakened Coop.

"Coop's awake," Henry said. "See there, Kid, I told you he wouldn't sleep through it all." He added a nervous laugh.

"What are you shooting at?" Coop asked.

"Well, it ain't rabbits." The Kid squeezed off another round.

"It has begun," Susan said as she came into the parlor. It was a statement, the words not spoken in fear. It could best be described as an observation.

"Yes," Coop said, "but as we said last night, if you women stay below the level of the windows, you should be quite safe. It might be better if you went back to one of the bedrooms."

"No," Susan said. "I'm staying right here. Alex needs me." She slid down against the wall as the shooting continued. Katherine and Elizabeth, with Minnie clinging to her mother's arm, sat down on the floor as well. The battle had begun.

Coop, realizing that Susan would not budge from her position, found an unmanned window and began exchanging gunfire with some of Peppin's posse.

Most of the men of the posse had positioned them-selves on a hill that had a good view of the McSween house. They began shooting but they were too far away for accurate marksmanship.

AFTER TWO DAYS of shooting back and forth, neither side had suffered any casualties, though the people of the town were staying in their homes, out of the line of fire. The McSween house was well provisioned and the women prepared food and supplied water for those inside the house. The men who had taken up their position in the stone tower didn't fare as well, and it was believed that they had abandoned the fight.

On the third day The Kid hit and severely wounded one of the deputies.

On the fourth morning, the army arrived from nearby Fort Stanton. Nine mounted black soldiers of the Ninth Cavalry and fourteen white infantrymen paraded down Main Street. They brought with them a Gatling gun, and a twelve-pounder howitzer which, if turned against the

McSween house could quite easily rip through the thick, adobe walls.

As the soldiers passed through the town, the men who were in Dolan's store, took advantage of the diversion. They moved to the house directly across the street from the McSween house and immediately unfurled a black flag, hanging it across the door.

"No prisoners," Coop said.

"What?" The Kid asked.

Coop pointed to the flag. "That was what Santa Ana used at The Alamo. A black flag means no prisoners will be taken."

"Yeah? Well, that can go both ways," Billy said.

The army made no overt effort to stop the fighting, but continued on through town to set up tents to establish their camp in an empty lot.

"I wonder what the army plans to do?" Coop asked.

"I don't know, but I'm not sure I trust them. Colonel Dudley sympathizes with James Dolan, which means if the army actually does get involved, it will be on the side of Pippen and his deputies," McSween said.

"We're badly outnumbered," Bowdre said.

"You aren't saying you want to surrender, are you, Charley?" Henry asked. "Because I don't know about you, but I don't want to wind up in no prison."

"No, I ain't sayin' nothin' 'bout surrenderin'," Bowdre said.

ONCE THE SOLDIERS passed through town Dolan's men took advantage of their new position to bombard the McSween house with gunfire. Within minutes they had shot out every window that was still intact. Bullets chipped away at the wooden doors and plunged into the adobe walls. Then, after one fusillade the shooting stopped and a man stepped out holding a white flag.

"Damn, they're wantin' to surrender," Bowdre said.

"No, that's Marion Turner. I'd say he wants to parley with us," Henry said.

McSween opened the door. "What do you want, Marion."

"I have warrants for everyone in your house," Turner said. "'N I'm callin' on you to surrender."

"We have warrants for most of your men as well," McSween said. "So I am returning the demand."

"What shall I tell the sheriff?" Turner asked.

Billy stepped into the door, cocked his pistol and aimed it at Turner.

"It don't matter. I'm goin' to kill you right here, 'n right now," Billy said in a menacing tone.

"What?" Turner replied, frightened at the sudden turn of events. "You can't do this! I'm here under a flag of truce!"

"Put the gun down, Kid," McSween ordered.

"Why? Ain't they're tryin' to kill us? This would just be one less of 'em." The Kid raised the gun to his shoulder.

"Put the gun down!" McSween shouted, and reluctantly, The Kid responded.

"Go back across the street, Marion. Tell George that our warrants are just as valid as his, and if he wants to stop the fighting, we can call it a stalemate. But we aren't going to surrender."

Turner looked at The Kid, with fear for his life still evident in his eyes, then he turned and hurried back across the street. Within a minute after he was back inside, the shooting resumed.

"So much for a stalemate," Coop said.

The shooting continued for what seemed like hours. Finally McSween turned away from his window.

"I'm going to go outside under a white flag and take a message to Colonel Dudley," he said.

"No, Alex, don't," Susan begged. "They'll shoot you."

"Not if I'm carrying a white flag."

"Oh? Do you think for a minute that Marion Turner wouldn't be dead if you hadn't stopped Billy from shooting him? What if there's no one to stop James Dolan from shooting you?"

"You're right of course, but someone should go see the colonel. The army is camped less than a quarter mile away. They're supposed to protect the citizens of this country, but yet this battle rages on." McSween's frustration was evident.

"We can send Minnie," Elizabeth Shield said. "Nobody is mean enough to shoot at a ten year old girl."

"That's it," Susan said. "Minnie can go. Honey, would you be willing to walk down to the end of the street and deliver a note to Colonel Dudley?"

"Yes, ma'am, I'll go."

"You aren't afraid?" McSween asked.

Minnie shook her head. "No, sir. Mama said they won't shoot a little girl."

"You're very brave Minnie," McSween said as he pulled the child to him. He held her for a minute blinking his eyes to keep a tear from forming. "I'll write a note for you to take to Colonel Dudley."

The note read as follows:

Why are you in town? Why have you not stopped the shoot-ing? Why are the soldiers surrounding my house? You have brought a howitzer with you. Is it your intention to blow up my house?

"Now wait for a moment until I call across the street," McSween said as he handed the note to Minnie. He stepped to the front door, opened it, and shouted.

"We're going to send a little girl out, and I'm asking you not to shoot her!"

"We ain't goin' to shoot a little girl," someone called back. "What kind of men do you think we are?"

"Coop, Henry, be ready," The Kid said, quietly. "If you see anyone aimin' at Minnie, be ready to shoot 'im."

"All right, honey. Go ahead," Elizabeth said.

Minnie Shield left the house and everyone held their breath as she walked down to the army encampment to deliver McSween's note.

They waited anxiously for several minutes, then Bowdre, who had been standing at the window called out.

"Here comes Minnie; a soldier's with her."

"It's Lieutenant Goodwin," McSween said.

"That's a good sign, don't you think?" Susan asked.

"We shall see."

Lieutenant Goodwin waited until Minnie was safely back in the house, then he started back toward the army encampment.

"What did Colonel Dudley say?" Susan asked, anxiously.

"He didn't say anything, he just wrote this note." Minnie handed the note to McSween.

McSween read it, then got red in the face. "He won't help."

Coop took the note from McSween's hand, then read it aloud.

"No soldiers have surrounded your house and I desire to hold no correspondence with you, McSween. If you wish to blow up your own house, that will be perfectly fine with me so long as you injure no soldier in the process."

CHAPTER 8

THE LULL IN GUNFIRE LASTED UNTIL LATE MORNING THEN Susan decided to take advantage of the break to go down to the river to get a bucket of water. That was when she saw two of McSween's employees taking wood from a nearby woodpile and stacking it against the east wing of the house.

"Sebrian, Miguel, what are you doing?"

"Sorry, Mrs. McSween, but these three men are forcing us to pile the lumber up here. I think they intend to burn your house down."

Sebrian pointed to three men who were standing behind them.

"Are you serious?" Susan asked the three men, all of whom were holding pistols. "Don't you know there are women and children in this house? Surely, you're not mean enough to set it on fire."

"Get back inside and mind your own business," one of them said as he turned his gun toward Susan.

When Susan got back inside she told the others what she had seen.

"You know this house is almost all adobe," McSween said. "It's not going to burn."

"Then why are they stacking wood against the house?" Susan demanded. "I'm going to go speak to Colonel Dudley."

"It won't do any good; you saw the note he sent."

"Minnie is just a little girl and all she could do was deliver the note. She couldn't plead our case with him, but I can and I will."

"If it comes to pleading a case, I should do it," McSween said. "I am the lawyer."

"Alex, you would be shot before you could get ten yards from the house. They didn't shoot Minnie because she's a little girl, and I don't think they'll shoot a woman. Besides, there's a pause in the shooting. Now's the time to go."

McSween sighed, and nodded. "All right, go ahead."

"Me 'n Henry will keep an eye open," The Kid said. "If we see anybody aimin' at you, we'll shoot 'im."

Susan laughed. "That's good to know." She moved to the door and stood there for a moment as if steeling herself for what she was about to do. Then she opened the door and marched boldly down the middle of the street, as if she were daring someone to shoot at her.

The soldiers looked at her with curiosity when she reached their bivouac.

"Where might I find Colonel Dudley," she asked a lieutenant.

"He's prob'ly in there, ma'am," one of the soldiers said, pointing to the lone Sibley tent.

When she stepped into the tent she gasped in surprise. Colonel Dudley wasn't there, but Sheriff Peppin was.

"What are you doing here?"

"I'm the sheriff of Lincoln County, and I'm responsible for maintaining the law in this town. As if this was any of your business, Mrs. McSween, I've come to coordinate operations with Colonel Dudley."

"Is it your intention to maintain the law by burning my house down?"

"If you don't want your house burned, you can move out all them men you're keepin' down there. By the end of this day, this thing's gonna be over, and I don't care how it ends. They can be dead or they can be alive; it's up to them. And believe me, you won't get any help from Colonel Dudley or anybody else you might go beggin'."

"Sheriff Peppin, I have spoken with . . ." Colonel Dudley was saying as he stepped back into the tent, but he paused in mid-sentence when he saw Susan. "Who are you?"

"I am Mrs. McSween. My husband, Alexander McSween, is a lawyer and a . . . ."

"I know who he is," Dudley said. "He's certainly not very courageous, is he? First he sends me a note by a little girl, now he sends his wife."

"Colonel, if you are here to protect us, I think you should know that this man," she pointed to Peppin, "and the men who are his deputies, are planning to burn my house down."

Dudley made no verbal response, but merely shrugged his shoulders.

"Didn't you hear what I said? Sheriff Peppin is going to burn my house down and there are people in it, including my sister and her daughter, whom you met, as well as

Miss Gates, the school teacher. Are you here to protect us, or are you here to support Sheriff Peppin?"

By now the four officers under Dudley's command had come into the tent to witness the meeting.

"I am not here to support anyone, which means that it is none of my business whether or not anyone burns down your house. And that is especially so, madam, as long as you harbor such men as the renowned outlaw known as Billy the Kid."

"Then why are you here?"

"I have just been informed by Sheriff Peppin that there are arrest warrants against the men in your house," Dudley said.

"Those arrest warrants are nothing more than death warrants," Susan replied. "And may I remind you that in April a court exonerated my husband and all the others."

"That is not my concern."

"Colonel Dudley, I have always had nothing but the highest respect and admiration for our military."

"Have you now? Well, I am so . . . pleased . . . to hear that." Dudley set the word "pleased" apart from the rest of the sentence to accent its sarcasm.

"You, you are a despicable human being! How were you ever commissioned an officer?"

"This, coming from someone who has no shame in identifying herself as Mrs. McSween?"

"Why should I feel any shame? I am proud to be Alex's wife!"

"Your husband, madam, is a man totally without principles. Why in this very missive that he wrote to me, he states that he is going to blow up his own house, with everyone in it." Colonel Dudley held up a paper to illustrate his point.

"What? I don't believe that! Alex would never write such a thing. Let me see that letter."

As Susan reached for the letter, Colonel Dudley slapped her hand away, doing it so powerfully that she cried out in pain.

"Lieutenant Fillion, if this woman reaches for this letter again, shoot her."

"Yes, sir," Fillion said, drawing his pistol.

"You don't understand, Colonel. Sheriff Peppin has no plans to arrest my husband or any of the other men. It is his intention to kill them."

"Is that all, madam?" Colonel Dudley said, dismissively.

"Yes, that is all. I must tell you," Susan said, her eyes narrowing, "your being in town today seems a little too thin, if you ask me."

"What did you say?" Dudley demanded, angrily.

"I find you and our crooked sheriff in collusion, and you say that you have no side, but by your very actions, you give lie to that statement."

"Lieutenant Fillion, escort this woman out of here. Madam, you may return to your house, for as long as it may stand."

SHORTLY AFTER SUSAN RETURNED, the shooting was renewed. The defenders kept an eye on the street, shooting at any of the posse that showed themselves. Because they were concentrating on what was before them, they were unaware that some members of the posse had managed to throw coal oil on the kitchen floor. They had ignited the coal oil, and smoke began drifting through the rooms as Elizabeth and Katherine attempted to douse the flames with a pail of water.

"They've done it! The house is on fire!" McSween said. "Get the women out of here!"

"No, Alex, I will not leave you." Susan's calm demeanor was in contrast to McSween's excitement.

"Susan, you've got to go," McSween pleaded. "We aren't going to stay here and burn up, but we can't be worrying about you."

"Alex is right, Mrs. McSween," Coop said. "It will be easier for us to deal with the situation if we know the four of you are safe."

"I appreciate your concern, Mr. Cooper, but the house is made of adobe.

You have said over and over that there isn't that much that can burn. I believe that to be true," Susan said. "I'm staying with my husband."

"It's your decision," Coop said as he turned his attention to the window he was manning.

It was then that he saw Jack Long and Buck Powell run up with more coal oil in an attempt to start a fire in another location.

"Here they come again!" Coop called and he, Henry and The Kid began shooting at them.

Long and Powell, caught by surprise, had no choice but to run to the nearest cover, which happened to be the outhouse.

"That outhouse ain't goin' to stop our bullets," The Kid said. "Fire away!"

BULLETS BEGAN POPPING through the walls of the outhouse and though none of them found their mark, Powell realized they were in a perilous situation.

"We ain't safe in here!" Powell said as he settled to the floor of the flimsy building.

"We sure as hell ain't safe outside," Long replied.

"What are we going to do?"

"Help me get this two-holer bench pulled up," Long said.

"What for?"

"We're goin' down in the pit."

"The hell we are! I ain't jumpin' in no hole that's full of shit," Powell said.

"Then stay up here 'n die," Long said as he jumped down into the hole. A bullet came so close to Powell that he jumped in as well.

THAT AFTERNOON, a cattle rustler who considered this attack to be against John Chisum instead of against McSween and the Regulators, piled wood shavings against a wall. When he was able to start this fire, it reached the board roof. Even though the roof was covered with dirt, the boards caught and began to smolder.

Several men attempted to run to the river to fetch more water, but the rustler and others from the posse rained bullets upon anyone who ventured out of the house. Soon the windows, door frames and furniture began blazing causing so much smoke that it was getting difficult to breathe.

"We need to get the women out of here," Coop said.

"How?" Elizabeth asked. "I think it has reached the

point where they would just as soon shoot us, as any of the men."

"I'll go see Colonel Dudley and beg him to rescue us," Katherine said.

"No, Katherine, they'll shoot you as soon as you step out into the street!" Susan warned.

"If we stay, we'll die of asphyxiation. I'd just as soon be shot."

"She's right," Coop said. "The only chance the women have is if Dudley comes for them."

"And what about Reverend Ealy and his wife?" Elizabeth asked. "They and their five children are in Tunstall's store. Who's to say that won't be the next target these madmen go after?"

"Before you leave, let me yell across the street," McSween said.

Once again McSween held a white flag out the door.

"Dolan," he shouted. "The school teacher's coming out. She's unarmed."

"Send her out," Dolan called back.

McSween nodded at Katherine, and taking a deep breath, she stepped through the front door, then, coughing, moved out into the street. Nobody shot at her.

The Kid watched through the window until he saw her enter a tent. "She's down at the army camp."

Minnie started an almost uncontrollable spasm of coughing as tears were rolling down her soot covered cheeks.

"Lie down on the floor and keep your nose as low as you can," Coop said. "That's where the air will be the cleanest."

Susan and Elizabeth joined Minnie on the floor.

"What Dudley will most likely do is just keep her there," The Kid said.

At that moment, a ceiling in the room behind them collapsed, causing the wall to fall as well. It barely missed the three on the floor.

"Surely, now that he knows the danger we're in, Colonel Dudley will send help," Elizabeth said as she crawled to another spot. The collapsing ceiling allowed much needed air to clear out some of the black smoke that was everywhere.

"I don't trust the son of a bitch," The Kid said. "Excuse the language, ladies."

"That's all right, Billy," Susan said. "Remember, I met the man. He *is* a son of a bitch."

The others laughed, providing them with the only bit of levity possible under the circumstances.

About fifteen minutes later, The Kid, who was still looking through the window hole, called out.

"I'll be damn! Here they come."

"Here who comes?"

"There's a solider drivin' a wagon, 'n Miss Gates is sittin' beside 'im. 'N there's a soldier ridin' escort on either side of the wagon."

The wagon stopped first in front of Tunstall's store. Katherine ran into the store, then reappeared a moment later with the Ealy family. Then the wagon stopped in front of the burning McSween house.

"Kiss your husband goodbye," The Kid said, "and then get out of here."

Elizabeth and Minnie ran out of the house and climbed into the wagon. Susan hung back. She embraced her husband reluctant to leave him.

"My sweet, sweet Sue," Alex said. "I know that you don't want to go, but you have to—for my sake. Know that I will always love you, and I will do what I can to stop this feud." He kissed her, and walked with her to the remaining door.

When Susan was aboard, the driver turned the wagon around, then drove it back to the encampment. The women and children were safe.

"THAT'S A RELIEF," Coop said.

"Yeah, but we're goin' to have to get out of here," Henry said.

"How?" The Kid asked.

"We'll wait 'till nightfall."

THE DEFENDERS WERE able to hold off any rushes against them, but as soon as night fell, they split up, slipping out into the darkness a few at a time, even as smoldering timbers and flashes of gunfire showed that bullets were still bombarding the house. A couple of hundred yards away from the McSween house, Coop, Henry, The Kid and George Coe saw several old barrels lined up against a wall. The four men clambered up on top of the barrels, then let themselves down on the other side.

By now they had gone two nights without sleep, and one full day without eating.

"What about McSween?" Coop asked. "I hate leaving him there alone."

"We give him the chance to come with us, 'n he wouldn't leave the house," The Kid said.

"When they find out nobody's shootin' back at 'em, they'll more 'n likely know that we've left," Henry said. "And I expect then they'll give up shootin' at the house 'n come lookin' for us."

"We can go to Ike Ellis's house," George Coe said. "He's my uncle."

"GEORGE! WHAT ARE YOU DOING HERE?" Ellis asked when the four exhausted men showed up at his back door. "I thought you might be with McSween."

"I was, and now we need a place to hide out for a spell."

"I'm sorry, George. You can't stay here. If Dolan finds out you're here, he'll have us all killed."

"We're hungry, Uncle Ike. And we don't have anywhere else to go."

"Ike, we can't turn them out without anything," Nancy Ellis said. "You boys come in; I'll get you something to eat."

"Thanks, Aunt Nancy."

Nancy Ellis took a smoked ham out of a cupboard. She cut all the meat off the bone and dropped it into a flour sack. Then she retrieved a half dozen biscuits that were under a cloth on the table and added those to the sack.

"I wish I had more to give you."

"This will dull the hunger," George said, anxious to get his hands on the sack.

"You're my own sweet sister's child, George, and I love you," Nancy said, "but Ike is right. You can't stay here." She was crying as she handed him the sack of food.

"I know we can't stay here, Aunt Nancy. And we thank you for helping us."

CLUTCHING the food that had been given them, Coop, Henry, The Kid and George left the Ellis house. They crawled on their hands and knees until they reached the bank of the Rio Bonito, then crossed the river on the narrow plank bridge.

"Let's destroy the bridge," The Kid suggested when they were on the other side. "It might slow the posse down a little if they're comin' after us."

"If any of the Regulators are still around, it might keep them from escaping if the bridge is gone," Coop said.

"To hell with anyone else." The Kid said. "In a situation like this, it has to every man for himself."

"Coop's right, Kid, we won't be abandoning our friends," Henry said.

"We prob'ly don't have no friends left in town anyhow," Coe said. "McSween said that when the army come they most all left."

The four men reached an elevated plateau some distance from town and there, they ate ravenously. After eating, the exhausted men lay down and slept through till dawn.

THEY MADE their way to the little town of San Patricio late that afternoon, shocking the residents who thought that the Regulators had been killed to the last man. During the night most of the remaining Regulators came straggling in, in twos and threes.

"We was told that you'd all skedaddled after the army come in," The Kid said.

"Who told you that?" Sam Smith asked.

"That's what McSween said."

"Yeah, well, little did he know. Anyhow, he's dead now," Smith said.

"He's dead?" Coop shook his head. "I thought after we left, they would quit shooting at the house."

"Oh, that ain't how they got 'im."

"What do you mean? What happened?"

"What he done is the damndest thing I've done ever saw. What he done was, he just took a Bible and held it against his chest, 'n started walkin' toward the house where Peppin's posse was at."

"What happened next?" Coop asked.

"Why, them sons of bitches didn't pay no mind to him not bein' armed or nothin', and it didn't mean nothin' that he was holdin' a Bible neither. They just commenced a' firin', 'n they filled him full o' holes."

"What about the women? They were safe with the soldiers when we left," Coop said.

"Yeah, they're still safe. I saw it with my own eyes when they moved 'em out to the fort, only thing was Miss Susan—she wasn't in the wagon. That's one strong woman," Sam Smith said.

"Did she see her husband fall?" Coop asked.

"Can't say, but one thing's for sure. She'll see to it McSween gets a decent burial."

"I'm sure she will."

CHAPTER 9

A MONTH LATER THE REGULATORS, STILL MARKED AS fugitives, asked Coop to write a letter to Colonel Dudley at Fort Stanton.

Dear Colonel Dudley:

I write to you as a representative of a group of men you may know as the Regulators, or perhaps, Wilson's deputies. The latter is a true appellation for we were, indeed, duly empowered deputies of the court, commissioned to find and bring to justice those men who murdered John Tunstall.

As we set out to do this, however, we were met by a body of men who were also legally deputized, though their commission seemed to exist only to prevent us from accomplishing our mission.

The result of two legally constituted bodies working at cross purposes has been disastrous, and a war has developed here in Lincoln County. It is time for this war to come to an end. We should settle our differences in reasonable and civil discussion, not by continued force of arms

We, the Regulators, are willing to enter into such discourse. If, however, a settlement cannot be reached, then we ask you in all fairness to take no side in this conflict. Do not send your soldiers against us for we have the right, and the will, to oppose you by force, and this we will do. Further, we will resist, by armed engagement, any hostile element whether military or civilian, that we feel would be infringing upon our right to live our lives in peace.

I am James Cooper, and though I am the author of this missive, I have written in consultation with, and the approval of all the undersigned.

J.G.Scurlock
James Cooper
Henry Brown
William Bonney
Charlie Bowdre
Jim French
Frank McNab
John Middleton
Sam Smith
George Coe

NOT TOO LONG AFTER Coop mailed the letter to Colonel Dudley, a detachment of cavalry arrived at Lincoln.

"Damn, the letter didn't work," Spurlock said when they learned of the soldiers in Lincoln. "They've come for us."

"I'm not so sure they have come for us," Coop said. "If so, why would they go to Lincoln? Surely they know by now that we were run out of Lincoln."

"We weren't run out of Lincoln," The Kid insisted.

"Really?"

"Really."

"Well, let's put it this way," Coop said. "They didn't exactly beg us to stay, now did they?"

"We was run out of town, Kid, plain 'n simple," Henry said.

"So, what do we do about it now?" Bowdre asked. "I mean if the army has come after us."

"I'll tell you what we do," The Kid said. "We set up an ambush 'n we kill 'em all. Ever' damn one of 'em."

"Have you lost your mind, Kid? You actually want to fight the whole U.S. army?" Charley Bowdre asked. "Well let me tell you somethin'. I tried that about fifteen years ago, 'n it didn't work out so well now did it? 'N I had the whole Confederate army with me."

"It's not a whole army," The Kid said. "Hell, it's just a detachment 'n we got as many as they got. We could set up an ambush 'n have most of 'em killed before they even knew we was there."

"If you're going to attack the army you'll have to do it without me," Coop said.

"I've known you for a long time, Cooper, 'n I ain't never knowed you to be a coward," The Kid said.

Coop bristled at the comment, and he turned to face The Kid. "Would you like to put my courage to the test?" He let his hand hang loosely over his pistol.

"Now hold on, hold on there, both of you," Henry said, interjecting himself in the quickly developing feud. "Both of you are my friends, 'n I don't want to see either one of you shootin' the other one. Or gettin' shot for that matter. I say you stop this now, before it goes any further."

"That's all right with me," The Kid said.

"It's all right with me as well," Coop said. "But I'm still not going to be a party to the ambush of a detachment of soldiers."

"I ain't either," Smith said.

"If you do it, you'll do it without me," Bowdre said.

"Doesn't seem all that smart of an idea to me, neither," Scurlock said.

"Then what are we going to do?" Jim French asked.

"I'm going back to Lincoln and see if I can't get my life put back together," George Coe said.

"I think I'll be movin' on, too," McNaab said. "I've always had a hankerin' to see Wyoming."

"I guess that means we're breaking up," Smith said.

"I reckon it does," Scurlock agreed. "Maybe that's for the best. What about you, Kid? Where're you gonna go?"

"I'm not goin' anywhere," The Kid sad. "I plan to stay right here 'n steal enough to make a living."

"Steal what?" Charlie Bowdre asked.

"Horses. Hell, Charlie Fritz teamed up with Dolan, didn't he? He's got more horses than he can manage, so I plan to take some of 'em off his hands. I'm broke 'n I need to make a living."

"I'm with you," Bowdre said.

"Me too," Fred Waite added.

"Henry? Coop?"

Coop looked over at Henry.

"I'm ready to leave New Mexico, but I could use a little moving around money," Henry said.

"Kid, it was one thing to kill when we were fighting against those who were trying to kill us," Coop said. "I'd be willing to ride with you for a while, but only as long as we're stealing horses. The first time there's a shooting, I'll be gone."

"Me too," Henry said.

"I don't see no need for shootin'," The Kid said.

"Then I'm with you. For now," Coop said.

"That'll be two of us," Henry added.

THEIR FIRST OPPORTUNITY came two weeks later. They had located an isolated range where Fritz kept fifty horses. They decided to take the horses in the middle of the night, believing that there would be less chance of encountering any of Fritz's cowboys.

It was quiet where they waited in the rocks. Coop could hear crickets and frogs, a distant coyote and a closer owl, but nothing else. He strained his ears in vain for the muffled sounds of any nighthawks, the drum of horses' hooves, the rattle of the saddle and tack. Then they saw not one rider but six, and they weren't merely watching over the horses, they were herding them.

"I'll be damn!" Henry said. "That's McCoy and Wilson. They don't ride for Fritz. They're Dolan's men. What are they doin' here?"

"I'll tell you what they're doin' here. They're stealin' the herd," The Kid said. "Only, we're goin' to steal it from them."

"We ain't likely to get through this without some shootin'," Bowdre said.

"Yeah, well, at least they aren't innocent cowboys," Henry said, justifying their action.

The men pulled their pistols, checked the loads, then waited.

The riders continued their ghostly approach, men and animals moving as softly and quietly as drifting smoke. Coop cocked his pistol and raised it.

"Hold it right there!" The Kid called out.

"What the hell?" one of the men shouted. "Who is it?"

"You're stealin' these horses. Ride away from 'em and there won't be no shootin'," The Kid said.

"What the hell! Shoot 'em down, shoot 'em down!" one of the would-be thieves shouted.

The riders pulled their pistols then and opened fire and though Coop had come into this venture hoping to avoid shooting, he had no choice but to return fire. One of the horse thieves dropped from his saddle and skidded across hard ground. All hell broke loose as flashes of orange light exploded like fireballs on the rocks.

Coop and the men with him were well positioned in the rocks to pick out their targets even in the dark. The horse thieves on the other hand, were astride horses that were rearing and twisting about nervously as flying lead whistled through the air and whined off stone.

"Let's get out of here!" one of the men yelled and he, and the two thieves who were still mounted, galloped away.

Coop had an excellent shot at one of the retreating men but he held fire. Some of the others with him did fire, but the riders rode out of pistol range; then it grew quiet, with the final round of shooting but faint echoes bounding off distant hills. A little cloud of acrid-smelling gun smoke drifted up over the deadly battlefield, the entire battle having taken less than two minute.

The herd of horses had been startled by the gunfire, but they hadn't broken into an absolute stampede as cattle might have done. Coop and the others mounted and started after the horses. From the original fifty, they were able to gather thirty-seven.

"All right, boys, if we can get a hunnert 'n fifty dollars for a horse, 'n we got thirty seven of 'em, why, that'd be . . . uh, what would that be, Coop?" The Kid asked.

"Five thousand, five hundred and fifty dollars," Coop said.

"Whoowee, how much money would that be for each of us?"

Coop took another moment for the computation then said, "Nine hundred and twenty-five dollars apiece."

Ten days later they sold the horses to John Hollicott, manager of the LS Ranch in Oldham County, Texas.

"Boys, this is just the beginning," The Kid said as they divided the money among them. "I've got bigger plans than this."

"I wish you luck, Kid, I really do," Coop said, "but this is it for me."

"You're stickin' with me, ain't you, Henry?" The Kid asked. "Or, are you 'n Cooper joined at the hip?"

"I think I'll stay with Coop," Henry said. He smiled. "But look at it this way. Without us, you'll have a bigger cut from your next job."

"Yeah," The Kid said with a big smile. "Yeah, it will be, won't it? All right, you two get out of here."

"Good luck to you," Henry said.

Coop chuckled. "I would say, 'stay out of trouble,' but that isn't going to happen, is it?"

"No, sir, with what I got planned, there's more 'n likely goin' to be a whole lot of trouble." The Kid laughed.

"Onliest thing is, we'll be causin' the trouble for the other folks."

Coop and Henry watched Billy the Kid and the others ride away.

"What do we do now?" Henry asked.

"One of the riders with Hollicott said Tascosa's turned out to be a pretty good place to stay. I think it's no more than ten miles east of here," Coop said. "What do you say we ride over and see what's there?"

Henry swung into his saddle. "All right. Tascosa, here we come."

CHAPTER 10

When Coop and Henry approached Tascosa, they were taken by the bucolic scene that was spread before them. In the distance, sheep were grazing and irrigation ditches coming from the Canadian River, watered gardens and orchards.

"Who would think this town has such a reputation for hell-raisin'?" Henry asked as the two moved on toward the main street.

"I guess the same thing could have been said about Lincoln until last summer," Coop said. "It's not the place— it's the people."

Henry laughed.

"What did I say that was so funny?"

"It wasn't what you said. It's just how you say it," Henry said.

"Well, then, let's just stop talking and find us a place to get a drink."

Tascosa was smaller than Lincoln, but it had more than its share of saloons. One of the easiest cattle crossings on the Canadian River was nearby, and nearly every ranch in the Southwest brought their herds through on the trail to Dodge City. Consequently, there were multiple saloons built to cater to the drovers, but at this time of year, the town was quiet.

Coop and Henry dismounted in front of the first saloon they saw. It was a small adobe building with a big sign attached to the roof.

"The Equity Saloon," Henry said reading the sign. "What in the hell does that mean?"

"The word has lots of meanings, but in this case it probably means they'll serve everybody with fairness."

"How do you know all this stuff, Coop?"

"I don't know, I just do. Come on, I'll buy you your sarsaparilla."

"Of course you will," Henry said as they entered the building.

There were half a dozen men inside, three standing at the bar, two sitting at one of the tables, and one man sitting alone. He stood out from the others not only because he was a solitary drinker, but also in his appearance. He was a relatively small man with rimless glasses, wearing a three piece suit. A round-topped Bowler hat was on the table beside him. He had thin, blond hair, and a moustache that was so pale and sparse that it could barely be seen.

A provocatively dressed woman of an indeterminate age approached the two as they entered.

"Well now, you're a couple of new fellas," she said, smiling. The smile displayed a missing front tooth.

"Nothin' new about us, Missy," Henry said. "We've been rode pretty hard in our day."

"My name's Lily. Come on in. You too, handsome," she

added, looking toward Coop. "Would you boys like to have a drink with me?"

"Thank you, Miss Lily. It would be our pleasure to enjoy a libation with you," Coop replied.

"Oh my, you sure do talk pretty," Lily said.

Lily led the two men to the bar. "Pete, I've got some new friends, here."

"Well, Pete, I'll have a beer and my friend will have a sarsaparilla," Coop said. "And give the lady a drink of her choice."

Lily's eyes widened as she looked at Henry. "You don't like beer?"

"I choose not to drink alcohol," Henry replied without further explanation.

As the drinks were poured, Coop paid for all of them.

"Well now, Mister, how is it that you get stuck with paying for your friend's sarsaparilla?" Lily asked.

"It's a little debt he owes me," Henry replied with a chuckle.

"You boys just passin' through, are you?" a man asked as he moved down the bar to stand beside them. He was a portly man, totally bald on top of his head. Unlike most of the others, he was clean shaven.

"That depends on whether or not we can find work here," Coop said.

"What kind of work you lookin' for?" the man asked.

"Since we are currently unemployed, I don't think we can afford to be too choosy."

By mutual agreement Coop and Henry had decided not to flaunt the money they had received as their part in the sale of the stolen horses.

The saloon patron finished the rest of his beer, then

wiped his mouth with his sleeve. "My name's Ernie Wallace. I manage the stage coach depot and I'm looking for someone to handle our stock. Would either of you want the job? Only thing is I can't take on both of you."

"Yes!" Henry said. "I'll take it."

"Is that all right with you, or would you two rather flip a coin for the job?" Wallace asked Coop.

"Mr. Brown spoke before I did," Coop said. "By rights, the job should be his."

"How soon are you willin' to start?" Wallace asked.

"I'll start as soon as I find some place to live."

"Mr. Brown, is it?"

"Yes, sir, Henry Newton Brown."

"Well Henry Newton Brown, if you want to use it, we've got a room down at the depot."

Henry smiled and extended his hand. "Well then, I reckon I'll come with you now." He turned toward Coop. "You don't mind me leavin' you on your own, do you?"

"I'll survive," Coop said. "Go, get yourself settled in."

"Looks like you'll be needin' a job now," one of the other saloon patrons said to Coop after Henry left. "What's your name?"

"Cooper."

"Mr. Cooper, do you know anything about cows?"

"I've been around a few," Coop said.

"I know the foreman for the CL spread's lookin' for help. His name's Mathis, Vernon Mathis. You could ride out and talk to him."

"Working on a ranch wouldn't be my first choice, but it may well be that circumstances will compel me to consider it."

"All right, but don't wait too long. Mr. Mathis needs

somebody quick, cause seems like half his hands are in jail."

"Can you cook, Mr. Cooper?" Lily asked.

"The only cooking I've ever done has been over a campfire, but if it comes down to it, I'd certainly be willing to give anything a try," Coop said.

"You might check with Jesse Sheets over at the North Star," Lily said. "I heard he was looking for a new cook."

"Actually, as far as that goes, I could probably use you around here," Pete said. "I mean cleanin' 'n such. That is unless you'd be a' thinkin' that a job like this would be beneath you."

"Pete, no man is above honest work," Coop said.

"Any man with that kind of attitude would be a good man to have workin for him," Pete said.

"You haven't told us what kind of job you'd like to have," Lily said.

"I . . . ," Coop started, then he paused for a moment before he continued. "I know it might sound a bit super-cilious of me, but I think I'd like a job that requires more intellect than muscle."

"Whoowee, super..., supersil..., I don't even know what that big word means but, like I said a' while ago, you sure do talk pretty," Lily said.

At that moment a loud peal of raucous laughter caused everyone to turn toward its source as three men pushed their way into the saloon.

"Did you see the look on Annie's face when I dropped that frog down the front of her dress? That's the funniest damn thing I ever seen!" one of the men said, and the others laughed.

"The sheriff didn't have no call kickin' us out of the

Cattle Exchange just playin' a little joke," one of the others said.

"LX men," Lily said under her breath. The tone of her voice suggested her disapproval of the new customers. "The big one is Duke. He's the meanest of the lot."

Coop looked over at Duke, who was a couple of inches taller and at least thirty pounds heavier than he was. And it was obvious that the extra size was muscle.

"He lords it over everyone because he's so big," she added.

"Hey, Pete," Duke called out as the three men stepped up to the bar. "How 'bout some o' that mule piss you try 'n pass off as whiskey in here?"

"If you don't like our whiskey, Duke, you're free to go someplace else," Pete said.

"Now just where 'n hell else is it that you are a' thinkin' that we can go?" Duke asked. "I mean, seein' as ole Clem here dropped a frog down between Annie's titties, 'n it got us kicked out of the Cattle Exchange."

"I'd just as soon none of you make any trouble in here," Lily said.

Duke looked at Lily and laughed. "Don't you be worryin' none, Lily, your pretty little titties are safe from us."

The other two men laughed, then reached for the glasses of whiskey Pete had poured for them. Picking up the glass Duke turned to look out over the saloon. His perusal stopped when he saw the small man sitting alone.

"Well now, lookie here," Duke said, lifting his glass to point. "Any of you boys ever see a more sissy lookin' man? I mean all dressed up in a suit 'n all. 'N with that little bitty hat layin' there on the table."

"Hat?" one of the other LX men asked. "You callin' that a hat, are you? Why, that ain't no hat. That's a piss pot. Hey, Mister, what's that piss pot doin' on the table? It's supposed to be kept under the bed."

The three LX men were the only ones to laugh at the joke.

"You know what? I think maybe we ought to make 'im pee in that piss pot, then put it on," Duke said. "Wouldn't that be funny?"

"Duke, why don't you and the boys just have your drinks real quiet like, and leave that man alone?" Lily asked.

"We ain't goin' to hurt 'im—we're just funnin' 'im," Duke said. Duke pulled his pistol and pointed it at the man who was still sitting at the table. "Now, little feller, what me 'n my friends want you to do is take out that little pecker of yours 'n pee in the piss pot you're callin' a hat."

Coop walked over to the table where the man was sitting.

"Hi," he said with a friendly smile. "Do you mind if I join you?"

"Mister, what the hell do you think you're a' doin', buttin' in like this?"

"Do you mind?" Coop asked in a conversational voice. "I'm trying to introduce myself to this gentleman."

"You damn right I mind," Duke said.

"Why don't you just enjoy your drink and allow this gentleman and me to enjoy a peaceful conversation?"

Duke walked over to the table and leaned down toward Coop, who had by now taken a seat.

"Why, I ought to . . ."

That was as far as Duke got before Coop pulled his pistol and brought it around sharply, hitting Duke in the face. The big man went down like a pole-axed steer, with blood pouring from his nose.

"Hey, what the hell are you . . ." one of the LX men yelled. He went for his gun.

"Tired of living are you?" Coop asked as he cocked his pistol and pointed it at the belligerent cowboy. "If you so much as touch that gun, Mister, I'll kill you."

The man jerked his hand away from the gun. "I ain't drawin', I ain't drawin'!" he shouted in a frightened voice.

By now Duke was sitting up, though he was still groggy. He put his hand to his nose then drew it away and looked at the blood that had pooled in the palm of his hand.

"What . . . what happened?" he asked.

"You fell down," Coop said. "Miss Lily, if you would please, this gentleman seems to be in need of a towel."

Lily reached over the bar to get a towel. "I'll give him this towel, but he sure ain't no gentleman." She tossed the towel to Duke, who immediately held it against his nose.

"You boys are about to be kicked out of another saloon today," Pete said.

"What you talkin' about? You ain't got no right to kick us out."

Pete reached under the bar then pulled out a double barrel, sawed-off shotgun.

"Yeah, I do," he said.

The two men looked at the two big holes in the end of the shotgun, then they helped Duke to his feet. Coop holstered his pistol as the three men left. Once they were gone, the remaining customers in the bar applauded.

"That was a good thing you done, Mr. Cooper," Pete said. "If you don't find the kind of job you're lookin' for, there's a place for you right here. You're a good man and I'd be proud to have you workin' here at The Equity."

"Thanks," Coop said. He looked across the table at the man who had been the unwelcome subject of Duke's attention. At the moment he was examining his hat,

"Lily?"

"Yes?"

"Would you please bring me another beer, and whatever this gentleman is drinking?" Coop pointed to the man who had been the butt of the cowboys' joke.

"I'd be glad to," Lily said.

"I hope you don't mind my barging in on you like this. You will share a drink with me, won't you?"

"Of course I will, and I'm happy to do so," the man replied with a smile. "After coming to my defense as you did, how could I refuse you?"

"Thank you," Coop said. "Are you all right?"

"I am, thanks to you, Mr. Cooper."

"You know my name?" Coop asked in surprise.

"I heard your name mentioned a minute ago. My name is Malone, Walter Malone."

"It's a pleasure meeting you, Mr. Malone. My friend and I just arrived in town today and, except for the three men who were just invited to leave, all of your neighbors in this town have been friendly."

"Yes, most of the people in this town are pleasant, aren't they? But they aren't my neighbors, as I, too, am a visitor to this town."

"Well, then, we have that in common."

Malone lifted his hat and turned it around. "What do you suppose those gentlemen found wrong with my hat?"

Coop laughed. "You are being quite generous in referring to those contemptible knaves as gentlemen. And I see nothing wrong with your hat, though I must say I don't believe I've ever seen a hat quite like that, at least not in the New Mexico Territory."

"It's quite dapper don't you think? It's called a Bowler, and I believe it is becoming quite popular among businessmen back East."

"Well, it's a fine hat, if you ask me," Coop said. "And as you are wearing it, one might deduce that you are a businessman."

"Your deduction is correct. I gathered from the conversations I have overheard, that you, my good man, are seeking employment."

"That would be correct."

"I have a feeling you may be just the person I'd like to hire."

Coop shook his head. "I've been in Tascosa less than half a day, and it has been suggested that I become a cowboy, a cook and a janitor. Now you're offering me a job as a store clerk, but I don't think that's the place for me, Mr. Malone.

"Please don't tell me you consider clerking in a store beneath you. Did you not say, earlier, that no man is above honest employment?"

"*Touché,*" Coop grinned, sheepishly. "I'm sorry. I guess my response to your generous offer did sound that way."

"What makes you think I'm looking for a store clerk?"

"I don't know, I suppose I just assumed, though I realize that assumption *is* the mother of many errors."

Malone laughed. "Assumption is the mother of many errors. Very good! Very good indeed! You do have a way with words, Mr. Cooper. Tell me, are you a man of letters?"

"I beg your pardon?" Coop replied.

"Well, now perhaps I'm guilty of making an assumption. But I can't help but believe that you are an educated man. Am I wrong?"

"I have some education," Coop said without being any more specific.

"You mentioned earlier that you would appreciate a job that would require more intellect than muscle. What I have to offer is just such a job. Are you interested?"

"Perhaps," Coop said.

"I'm the editor and publisher of the *Fort Worth Whig Chief*," Malone said. "And now I'm looking to employ someone to work for me."

"In the newspaper business?"

Coop paused for just a moment. Working for a newspaper would be a dream come true, but Fort Worth was in Tarrant County, and that was where he was wanted, dead or alive. Of course, in Tarrant County he was wanted as Jack Copley, not James Cooper, but there would still be people there who would recognize him.

"You seem to be hesitating in your response," Malone said. "Perhaps you are intimidated by the challenge of working on a newspaper?"

"No, sir, I can think of no job I would like more. It's just that I don't know about moving to Ft. Worth . . ."

"You misunderstand, Mr. Cooper. The job offer has nothing to do with Ft. Worth. I intend to start a newspaper in Tascosa, and here is where I would want you to work. I would stay with you until the paper was up and running, but then I would need to get back to Ft. Worth. You would be the managing editor."

"So I would be staying here—in Tascosa?"

"That's right, at least for now," Malone said. "My question is would you be willing to take such a position?"

Coop smiled happily; then reached out to grab Malone's hand. "Mr. Malone, you have just hired yourself an editor!"

"At the moment, Mr. Cooper, I have hired an assistant. It remains to be seen whether or not you will be an editor."

"I will be," Coop said, confidently.

CHAPTER 11

A WEEK AFTER COOP WAS HIRED A FREIGHT WAGON ROLLED into Tascosa with the equipment necessary to set up the newspaper.

"This is the first step in presenting the *Tascosa Pioneer* to the people," Walter Malone said as he and Coop unloaded a Washington Hand Press. "This baby came all the way from San Francisco."

"I had no idea there were so many fonts to choose from," Coop said as he opened one of the wooden crates and picked up some of the small pieces of metal. "Will we ever use all of these?"

"Not all the time, but there will be occasions when you want the page to look exceptionally beautiful. Then you'll make copy out of one font and headlines out of another. But the real place where you'll use your creativity is when you set the advertisements."

"Oh, yes, the advertisements," Coop said. "I'd almost forgotten about them."

Malone stopped what he was doing and stared at

Coop. "I can't believe you said that. If there are no ads, there's no paper."

"Yes, sir," Coop said fully aware that he had made a mistake.

"This week, we'll call on every business in town. Then we can gage whether Tascosa wants a newspaper or not."

COOP FOLLOWED Malone from business to business all up and down Main Street.

"Good afternoon, Mr. Ross, I'm Walter Malone and this is James Cooper." Charley Ross and his wife owned Ross's Millinery shop. "I have hired Mr. Cooper to work with me in getting the *Tascosa Pioneer* started. I think Coop, as his friends call him, will make the *Pioneer* the finest newspaper in all of the Panhandle."

"Tascosa has a newspaper?" Ross asked.

"Yes, sir, we do now," Coop said. "And just think about it, Mr. Ross, it will be your source of all the latest news. And it will be much more than just news from Tascosa. Why with the miracle of telegraph wires, we'll have news from all over the state, the country, and the entire world! Imagine being able to hold in your hand, the latest news from Ft Worth, St. Louis, New York, or even London and Paris."

"Oh, my, that would purely be somethin' awesome to have now," Mrs. Ross said, coming over to join the conversation and as she got caught up in the excitement Coop exuded.

"And here's another thing about having a newspaper," Malone added.

"Let's suppose you had something new to sell, something that you know your customers would want to buy if they knew about it. By advertising in the *Pioneer,* you can let everyone in town know everything there is to know about your merchandise, through the convenience of advertising. Wouldn't that be a wonderful thing though?"

"Oh, Charley," Mrs. Ross said turning to her husband. "We could tell them about the new shipment of hats we just got in from Philadelphia. They may be the most beautiful ladies' hats I've ever seen." Mrs. Ross paused. "But I wouldn't know the first thing about letting the women know just how pretty they are."

"You don't worry about that, ma'am" Coop said. "You just show me the hats and I'll write something for you."

"Now, how much advertising do you wish to buy?" Malone asked.

BEFORE THE END of the day, Coop and Malone visited every business establishment in town: Shelton's Drug Store, Wright and Farnsworth's General Store, Seewald Jewelry Store, Jesse Sheets' North Star Restaurant, Kimball's Blacksmith Shop, Reinardt's Store, The Cattle Exchange, The Equity Saloon, the Half Way Bar, the Exchange Hotel and others. The biggest account which was a full page ad came from the Howard-McMasters Mercantile.

After a few stops, Malone had hung back and allowed Coop to make the sales pitch. By the time the day was over, they had sold over sixty dollars' worth of advertising.

When they were back at the office Malone slapped Coop on the back.

"This was a fantastic day my boy. If we could do this well for the entire month, why we'd bring in more than two hundred dollars. But you know the money won't always be this good unless you put out a paper that the townspeople will want to read."

"I'll do it, Mr. Malone, you can count on that."

"Oh, I *am* counting on it," Malone said. He smiled. "You know you've worked for me for a week and you haven't asked about your compensation."

"No, sir, I haven't." Although he didn't say the words aloud, the truth was he was so excited about the prospect of actually publishing a newspaper that he hadn't even thought of how much money he might make. But now that Malone had mentioned it, he was interested.

"You'll be responsible for your own salary," Malone said.

"Oh?"

"Once the paper is established, I'll take sixty dollars per month no matter how much the paper earns," Malone said. "You'll pay yourself and meet all the expenses from whatever remains of the money that comes in. Does that sound reasonable to you?"

"Yes, sir," Coop replied, excited by the new venture, "especially considering that we brought in sixty dollars in one day."

Malone laughed. "Remember what I said. It won't always be this way. There'll be a snowstorm in January where nobody leaves their house for a week, or a herd will come through and the drovers will be spending so much money, no one will think they need to advertise ever again. The key to success is what you write—make it good and the paper will survive."

A FEW DAYS LATER, after Coop learned how to use the press, the first issue of the *Tascosa Pioneer* was printed.

Hello Tascosa

In this, our very first issue, I would like to introduce you to your newspaper, the Tascosa Pioneer. Yes, I say that this is your newspaper for it will allow you to keep up with all the news of the city, state, nation, and the world.

I am James Cooper, or Coop as I am known, and I am the editor of the Tascosa Pioneer. Although I am a recent arrival, in the coming days as I begin to gather the local news, I hope to meet and become friends with all of you. I also invite you to use the newspaper to let your friends and neighbors know of any social engagement or community activity that you may be planning. In addition, this paper will be the means by which our merchants will be able to communicate directly with their customers, which of course will benefit you, our readers, for you will know what each advertiser has for sale, whether it is merchandize or a service that you may need.

And finally, may I suggest that you save this, the very first issue of the Tascosa Pioneer, (I have mentioned the name many time because I don't want you to forget it), for it is certain that in the days to come, this first issue will become a collector's item.

HENRY BROWN HAD BEEN WORKING for the stage coach line

for two weeks. He was moving the horses into the holding pen, getting them ready to attach to the coach that would be making the morning run to Dodge City. He had just put the last horse in the pen when Ernie Wallace came out to speak to him.

"Brown, do you know how to shoot a gun?" Wallace asked.

Henry was somewhat concerned by the question. Did Wallace suspect him of something?

"Yes, I know how to shoot a gun," Henry replied, reluctantly. "Is there any particular reason why you want to know?"

"Yeah, there's a reason. I just fired Leon Taylor 'cause he's drunk again. I can't have a shotgun guard who can't handle his liquor, especially when there's a big money shipment coming back from Dodge. Do you think you can take over for him?"

"You want me to ride shotgun on a shipment of money? Is it a very large shipment?"

"As a matter of fact, it is. And that's why I can't trust Taylor to make this run."

"Make shotgun guard a permanent position and I'll go," Henry said.

Wallace nodded. "All right, the job's yours. Oh, uh, and if you don't mind, would you go ahead and get the team changed out when the coach arrives? Just this one last time I mean, 'cause I don't have anyone else to do it right now. But I promise, I'll have somebody to take your place by the time you get back."

WHEN THE COACH arrived from Dodge City, Henry

changed the team. He had just gotten the new team in harness when he saw Eli Jacob coming toward him. Jacob was the driver.

"The team's hitched up and ready to go," Henry said.

"Good," Jacob said. "Wallace tells me you're going to be riding shotgun on this run."

"Yeah, but it'll be for more'n just this run. He's hired me full time."

"Good enough. It was gettin' to where Taylor was drunk more 'n he was sober anyway. If you gotta take a piss, better do it now. Our passengers are ready 'n we'll be leavin' in about five minutes."

"I'm ready to go," Henry said.

A few minutes later the three passengers came out of the depot and climbed into the coach. All three were men in their mid-thirties, and dressed in accordance with their trade. They were salesmen who had been in town to make calls on all the Tascosa businesses.

Henry used the front wheel to climb up onto the box and take his place as the shotgun guard. Jacob came up from the other side, picked up the reins and, holding them in his left hand grabbed the bull whip and popped it over the head of the team as loudly as if it were a pistol shot.

The horses lurched forward, and they were underway.

"How long's this trip?" Henry asked.

"Thirty four hours," Jacob answered.

"Thirty four hours? Damn, that's a long time."

"What do you have to complain about?" Jacob answered. "I'm the one drivin'. All you got to do is sit there."

Henry chuckled. "Yeah, let's hope that's right."

THEY MADE the trip to Dodge City without incident.

"Where's old Leon?" Ted Anderson, the Dodge stage coach manager, asked.

"He was drunk when we left," Jacob said. "He won't be ridin' with me anymore. This here's Henry Brown; he's the new guard."'

"Good to meet you, Brown," Anderson said, extending his hand. Henry took it.

"So, Jacob was drunk was he? Well, what's new about that? But it's good Ernie found somebody else," Anderson said. "Mr. Matthews down at the bank told me he'd be sending thirty thousand dollars through, 'n that's enough money to draw out the worst of 'em."

"Tell Mr. Matthews he has nothin' to worry about," Henry said. "We'll get the money through for him."

"Well now, for a new guy, you're sure full of piss and vinegar ain't you, Mr. Brown?"

"You want the money to get through, don't you?"

"Yes."

"Then you need someone who's full of piss and vinegar to see that it's done."

Anderson laughed. "Oh, indeed I do. I like your new man, Eli."

"Yes, we're lucky to have him. So, do we start back the same time as usual?" Jacob asked.

"Same as usual, twelve hour rest for driver and guard. Oh, by the way, there's a no gun law in Dodge, Mr. Brown, so you'll have to leave your pistol and shotgun here until time to go back," Anderson said.

"That's all right, I don't plan on shootin' anybody anyway. All I want to do now is get a good meal, a drink or two, then get some sleep."

"The company pays for meals at the Dodge House, and we also keep a room there that you 'n Eli will share." Anderson smiled. "But the drinks will be on your own."

"You goin' to have a drink, Eli?" Henry asked Jacob.

"I'll join you soon as I get the mail pouch turned in," Jacob said, holding up the canvas bag. "Anyway, I thought you told me you didn't drink."

"Oh, I drink all right. I mean, you don't expect me to pour the sarsaparilla in through my ear, do you?"

Jacob laughed out loud. "No, I don't reckon I do."

Henry nodded, then walked a couple of blocks down Front Street to the Long Branch. The saloon was alive with conversation and laugher.

"Sarsaparilla," Henry said when he stepped up to the bar.

"Sarsaparilla? Are you joking, Mister?" the bartender replied.

Henry stared at the bartender with an austere expression on his face. "Do I look like I'm joking?"

"No, I reckon not."

The bartender drew the sarsaparilla and set it in front of him.

"Do you know Eli Jacob, the stagecoach driver?" Henry asked.

"Yeah, I know 'im, but he ain't in here right now."

"I know, but he will be in a few minutes. I'll be sittin' at that table back under the elk's head. When he comes in, point me out to him, will you?"

"What's your name?"

"The name's Brown, but he already knows that. He's supposed to meet me and I just want to make it easy for him to find me."

"All right," the bartender agreed.

Henry carried his drink back to the table, then studied the saloon. The bar was long, and white, with a brass foot rail. There was a mirror behind the bar and above the bar an even larger set of antlers than the ones over Henry's head.

". . . thirty thousand dollars," someone said who was sitting at the next table over. He spoke quietly, but Henry was able to hear it. And because that was the same amount of money Ted Anderson had mentioned and it seemed unlikely that it would be a coincidence, the conversation got Henry's attention.

"That's a lot of money."

"Yeah, it is."

"Will you shut the hell up about it? What's the matter with you two? Have you gone loco or somethin'?"

"We was just commentin' on how much money thirty thousand dollars is, is all."

"Yeah, well keep your mouths shut about it."

The man who had admonished the other two glanced over toward Henry, who was staring at his glass of sarsaparilla.

"Come on, let's get out of here." The man rose from his seat, scraping the chair against the floor.

"Just hold your horses, I ain't finished my beer yet," one of the three men complained.

"Leave it. You can buy another one over at Hoovers."

Henry studied the three men as they left the saloon. Soon after they left, Jacob came in.

"I checked over at the Dodge House. They're roastin' a pig for supper tonight."

"Then that's what's been smellin' so good," Henry said.

"It not only smells good—it is good. They roast a porker ever' couple of weeks."

"Eli, have you ever been held up by road agents on any of your trips up here?"

"I've been stopped a couple of times. They get a trinket or two from the passengers, but I ain't never lost anything of value," Eli said. "Hell, most of the time we ain't carryin' anything worth stealin'."

"Except this time."

"Yeah, except this time," Jacob said.

"Have you ever carried this much before?"

"Shh," Jacob said, glancing around the saloon to see if anyone was listening. It didn't appear that anyone was. "As far as I know, I ain't never had this much. 'N that's why I'd just as soon keep this a secret."

Henry started to tell him it wasn't a secret any longer, but he withheld the information.

CHAPTER 12

Coop took it upon himself to be a promoter of both Tascosa and Oldham County. One of his earliest issues did just that:

OLDHAM COUNTY

So named for Captain Oldham, an early frontiersman, Oldham County is situated on the west boundary line of the state, bordering New Mexico, near the extreme northwestern corner of the panhandle. It has an area of 1,477 square miles, being more than half as large again as either of the other two organized counties in the panhandle, and as large as any of the unorganized counties in the area.

The general surface of this county, as of all the western and northwestern portion of the panhandle, is high, undulating prairie which is in some parts mountainous, with a diversity of fair valley and level plains. Along the rivers and their tributary creeks, are growths of cedar, cottonwood, hackberry, wild china berry, and mesquite.

There is ample grass for grazing and soil that promises much for farmers. Indeed much of the soil comprised in the famous staked plains will one day be converted by the wand of the actual settler. The mystic energies of the man with the hoe shall bring forth farms that one day will wave with yellow grain where now stretches only unbounded level, rich, soil.

But the prime interest of our section, the chief industry upon which thousands of our people depend at present and will for years to come, is stock-raising. The panhandle proper represents an ownership of somewhere near a million head of cattle, horses, and sheep. These animals find good winter grazing and sufficient protection in the valleys and gorges. Running water is unfailing in the driest of times due to the Canadian River, and the creeks flowing into it.

But what is needed, and what will be promoted by this newspaper to the mutual benefit of all parties, is rail service. To the railroad company that sees the marvelous benefits of bringing the iron horse to our locale will befall abundant benefits. Railroad profits will be generated by providing the shipment of our livestock to the markets, as well as the transport of needed goods and supplies to an eager base of consumers who here reside. Add to this the advantage of an active passenger service which, while generating additional revenues for the railroad, will bring new settlers to grow the market base even larger, and both area and railroad will be rewarded.

As long as this paper shall exist, and as long as the blood flows through the veins of the hand that pens these words, it will be the personal mission of the editor of the Pioneer to secure a railroad for the betterment of Tascosa.

"COOP, that was one fine article you wrote for the newspaper," Pete Cahill, the bartender at the Equity Saloon said. He drew a mug of beer and set it in front of the editor. "This first beer is on the house."

"Why, thank you, Pete," Coop said. Lifting the mug, Coop blew away the head, then took his first swallow. It tasted good, after having spent a long day in the press room, setting the type, then printing the paper. He wondered if the paper would ever be profitable enough to hire someone to assist him.

"Well, now, if it ain't the newspaper man," a chiding voice said. "Yes sir, here he is, a stranger that's come into our town 'n made hisself famous with all them fancy words he writes."

The bellicose words came from Duke, the same LX ranch hand Coop had encountered on his first day in town.

"I'm glad to see you've taken notice," Coop said, lifting his beer in salute.

"You snuck up on me last time," the big man said. "You won't be able to do that now, 'cause I'm a' watchin' you."

"You're watching me? Is some sort of performance expected?"

A few of the others laughed nervously.

"Whut?"

"I was just asking why you were watching me. Do you want me to sing? Perform a bit of prestidigitation? Do some juggling, perhaps?"

There was more laughter this time, and with less nervousness.

The expression on Duke's face grew even more confused.

"Whut?" he asked again.

"I'm sorry, Mr. Duke. I seem to have exceeded your capacity for comprehension."

Now the laughter of the others was universal.

The expression on Duke's face changed from confusion to anger. It was obvious that he had no idea what Coop was saying to him, but he was well aware that he was the butt of their laughter.

Duke held his arm out, pointing at Coop. "Me 'n you's goin' to get this settled right now," he said loudly, and with spittle flying from his mouth.

"Duke, Coop ain't heeled," Pete said. "And you ain't doin' nothin' 'till you shuck out of that gun." Pete backed up his statement with the shot gun that he took from under the bar.

"I don't need no gun to whup his ass," Duke said, unbuckling his gun belt and handing it off to the man who had come in with him.

"Are you ready, Mr. Newspaper man?" Duke asked.

"Try the experiment," Coop said.

"What does that mean?"

"It means that I'm ready to fight if you are."

Duke smiled broadly, then looked over at the others in the saloon.

"Did you hear that? The newspaper man is real . . ."

Coop hit Duke in the chin in mid-sentence. Duke staggered back and Coop stepped in to hit him again, this time in the stomach.

Duke, who won most of his fights by intimidation, was startled, not only by Coop's willingness to fight, but by the power in his punches. He backed away, but Coop gave him no chance to get his bearings. A combination left and right staggered him again and, desperately, Duke put his head down and charged, swinging.

One of Duke's wild punches connected, but the big man was unable to follow up as Coop avoided the next swing, then counterpunched with a blow to Duke's kidney. Duke gasped then moved in attempting to grab Coop in a clinch hold, but Coop hit him with a short right that stopped him cold.

The other saloon patrons were shocked by how the fight was going. They were used to seeing men back down to Duke or, barring that, Duke defeating them quickly. This fight was still going and while Duke was gasping for breath, Coop appeared calm and collected.

In a desperate move Duke charged again, swinging wildly, counting on his size and strength to, as it always had, prevail. Duke landed a solid right and, smiling, he stepped back to allow Coop to fall to the floor, but Coop didn't fall. Instead he threw a hard counterpunch which hit the big man in the nose, and it started blood gushing down over his mouth and chin.

The expression on Duke's face was one of shock, not only that Coop had not gone down before his best blow, but that he seemed to be losing this fight. Duke gave up any idea of using his fists and rushed toward him intending to use strength and size to grab Coop and throw him down. Instead, Coop used Duke's imbalance, to grab him by the front of his shirt and then jerking him forward, tripping him up with an extended leg.

Duke lay on the floor for just a moment, and Coop backed away to let him get up. Then, when Duke was on his feet again, Coop started toward him but Duke held out his hand and shook his head.

"I don't want to fight no more," he said.

"I'm glad to hear you say that," Coop said, "because I would just as soon not fight any more either. Go out to the watering trough, get your face cleaned up, then come back in here and have a beer, on me."

"No, hell no," the bartender said. "He won't be havin' a beer on you."

"Pete?" Coop asked, surprised by the bartender's comment.

Pete smiled. "Ever' body in the house will be havin' a drink on *me*," he said.

With cheers, everyone rushed to the bar.

FIFTEEN MINUTES later Duke and Coop were sharing a table.

"How come it is that you can fight like that?" Duke asked.

"I was a pugilist in college."

"Whut?"

"I was a prize fighter once," Coop said. It wasn't an accurate statement, but it was one that he knew Duke would understand.

"I'll be damn," Duke said. He smiled, then held up his beer. "That makes me feel better. I was some embarrassed about bein' beat up by a newspaper man, but bein' as it was a prize fighter that whupped me, it ain't so bad."

Coop raised his glass to touch Duke's. "I think you and I could call a truce now, don't you think? I mean no more fighting?"

"Yeah," Duke promised. "Startin' right now."

To Coop's surprise, Duke stood up then and turned toward the others in the saloon.

"Hey!" he shouted loudly. "Ever' body in here listen to me, 'cause I got somethin' I'm a' wantin' to tell you."

Duke pointed to Coop. "This here feller whupped me good 'n proper, 'n now we've made us a truce, so there ain't goin' to be no more fightin' betwixt us. 'N 'n I don't want to hear nobody sayin' nothin' bad about him no more."

"No how," Coop said.

"Whut?"

Coop chuckled. "I just wanted to see if I could get another negative in there."

"Oh."

"And, Duke, now that you and I won't be fighting anymore, I would appreciate it if you would be nice to my other friends, such as Pete, and Lily, and Scotty, and Joe, and some of the others."

"You got a lot of friends," Duke said.

"I do indeed, but that's necessary. If I didn't have a lot friends to support the newspaper, it wouldn't make it."

"Yeah, all right. I'll be nice to all of 'em. Where's your other friend?"

"My other friend?"

"The one you come to town with."

"Oh, you're talking about Henry Brown. Well, Henry's the new shot gun guard for the stage coach company, and I expect he's starting back from Dodge City about now."

CHAPTER 13

HENRY PUT HIS SHOTGUN UP IN THE BOOT OF THE DRIVER'S box and was standing by the coach as the three passengers came out of the depot to board. He had already been given the information about the two men and one woman. Chris Poindexter and Tom Byrd were cattlemen from near Tascosa. The woman was Ella Sheets, the wife of Jesse Sheets who owned the North Star Restaurant in Tascosa. She smiled at Henry and he held out his hand to help her climb aboard.

"Thank you," she said.

"You're welcome, Mrs. Sheets. I hope you have a pleasant trip back."

Henry climbed up beside Jacob.

"Everyone aboard?"

"Yeah."

"Heah!" Jacob called, accenting the shout with a loud pop of his whip. The stage headed down Front Street, its departure watched by many of the citizens of the town.

Henry studied the faces of all those who were watching the departure. He was looking for the three men he had overheard talking in the Long Branch last night, but he didn't see any of them.

The trail started at Dodge City and ran south to Brown's Soddy in Meade County, Kansas. It then crossed the Kansas-Oklahoma border near Hines Crossing on the Cimarron River. From there it turned southwest toward Beaver, Oklahoma. They drove on through the night with Henry and Jacob spelling each other on the reins so that each could get in a nap.

Eli had said that Leon Taylor had sometimes driven for him, and Henry gladly took his turn on the way up to Dodge City. It was the first time he had ever handled a six-horse team, but the horses were experienced and they knew the trail, so all Henry had to do was sit there, hold the reins, and try not to doze off.

He was certain the three men he had overheard planned to rob the coach; the only question was, would they do it during the night? That thought helped him stay awake, even as he listened to Jacob's snoring.

He also thought about the woman passenger who, like the others, was probably sleeping now. He knew both Ella and Jesse, and he knew that she was a dutiful wife to Jesse. More than likely she had come to Dodge City on some business for the North Star, because she was truly his partner in the marriage and the restaurant. He wondered what it would be like to be married to a woman like Ella, someone who was pretty, and someone who would share his life.

Could he ever live such a life?

He thought about his new job as shotgun guard. Today he might well prevent the robbery of thirty thousand dollars. What made that relatively unusual was if the men did attempt to hold up the stage, Henry realized that there wasn't that much that separated him from the robbers. So far he had lived a life just skirting along the edge of the law, moving back and forth across the line. He had engaged in cattle rustling and horse stealing. He had also been in several gunfights, and there had been times when he could have just as easily been killed, as survive.

His thoughts were interrupted by Jacob coughing, and clearing his throat.

"You awake, or are you just sittin' there hangin' on to the reins while the horses is doin' all the work?" Jacob asked.

Henry chuckled. "I'm awake, but the horses are doin' all the work."

"Gettin' light in the East," Jacob said. "It'll be sunrise soon, 'n we can have breakfast at the Little Blue."

"I sure would like a stack of flapjacks," Henry said. "And some bacon."

"Coffee will be good too," Jacob added as he reached for the reins.

TEN MILES SOUTHWEST of where Henry and Jacob were discussing breakfast, the smell of coffee permeated the campsite on a small stream that was a tributary to the Canadian River.

"Coffee smells like it's about ready," LeRoy Purvis said.

"It's ready," LeRoy's brother, Gil replied as he poured a cup for himself.

"Too bad we don't have no biscuits 'n bacon to go with it," Amon Hazel said.

"And gravy," Gil added.

"Breakfast will be coffee and be glad for it," LeRoy said. "You want to fill your bellies, think about the thirty thousand dollars we're about to grab. That'll be ten thousand apiece."

"Yeah," Gil said. "You know what I'm goin' to do with my money? I'm goin' to Memphis 'n I'm goin' to get on one o' them river boats 'n I'm goin' to play poker. Why, with this much money to back me, I'll double it a' fore I get to New Orleans."

LeRoy laughed. "You're a damn fool, Gil. You won't even make it to New Orleans. You'll have it all lost a' fore you get to Vicksburg. Then the next thing you'll more'n likely do, is, you'll come around my saloon, wantin' money from me, 'n thinkin' I'll give it to you, just 'cause I'm your brother."

"What saloon?"

"The one I'm goin' to buy up in Abilene. I'm goin' to have good whiskey 'n bad women." LeRoy and the other two laughed.

"What about you, Amon? What are you goin' to do with your money?" Gil asked.

"I'm goin' to go to LeRoy's saloon 'n then I'm goin' to spend ever' cent of it on that good whiskey and them bad women," Amon replied.

"Well now, see there, LeRoy, if Amon spends all his money with you, you'll have plenty to give me if I come around," Gill teased.

"You two boys finish your coffee and get saddled," Le Roy said. "I know the spot where we're goin' to stop the stagecoach 'n I want to be there in plenty of time to be ready."

HENRY and the others were having breakfast at the Little Blue stage station. It wasn't flapjacks as he had wanted, but the ham, eggs, potatoes and biscuits were satisfying enough.

"I tell you what, Mrs. Sheets. This is good food, but you 'n Jesse have it beat all hollow at the North Star.

Ella Sheets' smile caused her dimples to show. "Well, that's very sweet of you to say, Mr. Brown."

"All right, folks," Jacob said a few minutes later. "We've got a new team hitched up, 'n it's 'bout time to go."

At the Little Blue stage station the trail branched, and they took the northern branch which led to Tascosa by way of Hartley County. Having come up by the same trail a few days earlier, Henry knew exactly where all the points were that would be the best place to jump the coach, but so far nothing had happened. He was beginning to think that they might just be lucky enough to make it all the way to Tascosa without any trouble. Then they were approaching a rather sharp curve to the west. On the left side of the road there was a ridge line that could provide cover for anyone lying in wait.

Henry was not only aware that this was the last opportunity any road agents would have to be able to remain out of sight until the last minute; he suddenly felt a chill in his body, and he knew that this is where it was going to happen. He didn't know how he knew, but he was as certain as he was that the sun was in the sky, that they were about to be hit.

"Get ready," Henry said.

"Get ready for what?" Jacob asked, surprised by the unexpected comment.

"If we're going to be hit, it's going to happen right up ahead of us where the road makes a curve to the right."

"We've passed dozens of places better 'n this one for any robbers to hide," Jacob said. "Just what makes you think we're going to be hit here?" He chuckled. "Gettin' a little nervous are you? I mean what with this bein' your first trip 'n all."

"Would you rather me be sleeping?"

"No," Jacob said. "No, sir, Henry, I have to admit that you've got yourself a point there."

Although Jacob didn't see him do so, Henry pulled his pistol, held it down by his side, and pulled the hammer back.

"Now that I think about it, I reckon I do like a man that takes his job serious," Jacob said.

Just before the coach reached the curve Henry had pointed out, three mounted men suddenly rode out from behind the ridge. All three were wearing face masks, and all three were carrying rifles. They stopped in the middle of the road.

"Hold it right here!" the one in the middle shouted, holding up his hand.

"Woah!" Jacob shouted, hauling back on the reins and pushing the brake lever forward. The coach came to an abrupt stop.

"Throw down that bank pou . . ."

That was as far as he got before Henry opened fire. He shot three times, the gunshots coming right on top of each other. Henry purposely chose the outside two men to fire at first because they had both hands on their rifles, whereas the man in the middle did not. He had raised one hand to stop the stage.

"Son of a bitch!" Jacob shouted in both shock and fear.

Henry snapped off his final shot and the one in the middle went down as well. Now, all three of the road agents were lying in the dirt, two of them face down and the third face up to the sun. From his position in the driver's box, none of the three appeared to be moving.

"What's happening? What's going on up there?" one of the men from in the coach called. "What's the problem?"

"There's no problem," Henry called back calmly, as he climbed down from the stage to have a closer look at the three men he had just shot.

Henry removed the masks, but it wasn't necessary. He knew before he looked, that these would be the same men he had overheard talking in the Long Branch Saloon, back in Dodge. And his suspicion was correct.

By now the three passengers from the coach approached slowly, and cautiously.

"It's all right, they're all dead," Henry assured them.

"I'll be damn," Chris Poindexter said when he was close enough to see them. "I know these men. At least, I know two of them. That one in the middle is Leroy Purvis, and that one to his right is his brother, Gil. They used to ride for me 'till I fired them both for stealin' cows from me. I don't know who the other man is though."

"I tell you the truth, I never seen nothin' like this before!" Jacob said, talking excitedly. "I mean them three men threw down on us, 'n ole' Henry here, why he shot all three of 'em a' fore you could say Jack Robinson. 'N I mean that was with them men already with their guns in their hands."

The woman passenger didn't approach the three bodies, but remained inside the coach. Henry walked back to check on her, and saw an expression of horror on her face.

"Are you all right, Mrs. Sheets?" he asked.

"Yes," she said quietly. "I just wasn't expecting such a thing."

"No, ma'am," Henry said. "I don't expect any of us were."

"Do you think anyone would mind if I stay in the coach? I would just as soon not look at them," Mrs. Sheets said.

"You just stay where you are, ma'am." Henry walked back up to the front of the coach where the others were still staring down at the dead, would-be robbers.

"Is Mrs. Sheets all right?" Jacob asked.

"She's fine."

"What are we goin' to do with these men?" Tom Byrd asked.

"What do you mean, what are we going to do with them?" Poindexter replied. "There's nothin' to do with 'em now; they're dead."

"Yeah, but we can't just leave 'em lyin' here. This is a public road," Byrd said.

"Mr. Byrd's right," Henry said. "We can't just leave 'em here."

"I'll tell you what we're goin' to do," Jacob said. "We're goin' to put these sonsofbitches belly down on their own horses 'n take 'em on in to Tascosa with us."

"How will we know who belongs on which horse?" Byrd asked. "The horses is likely to get a little skittish if he don't get 'em matched up right."

"That's easy enough," Poindexter said. He pointed to two of the horses. "Those are my horses, stolen from me by the Purvis boys. That means this fella belongs on that horse," he said, pointing out the third man.

"All right, let's get them slung over the saddles so we can get on our way," Jacob said, taking charge of the situation.

With two men to each body, it took less than a minute to get the dead robbers loaded, then everyone climbed back onto the coach and they got underway.

"How much longer?" Henry asked.

"We'll be there by mid-day."

Absolutely certain that there would be no further attempts, Henry slumped down on the seat and watched the bobbing heads of the six horse team that pulled the coach along at a steady five miles per hour.

Thirty thousand dollars, he thought. Thirty thousand dollars is a lot of money. What couldn't I do with thirty thousand dollars?

"Damn," Henry said aloud, and he reached for the canteen.

Jacob chuckled. "That dust will get to you, won't it?"

"Yeah," Henry said, not giving voice to his thoughts. He took a long swallow of water and willed thoughts of the thirty thousand dollars out of his mind.

CHAPTER 14

BY LATE MORNING, A COUPLE OF COWBOYS FROM A NEARBY ranch saw the stage on its way to Tascosa. When they saw the bodies draped across the three trailing horses, they rode over to take a look.

"Hey, them's the Purvis brothers," one of them said. "I know them boys; they used to ride for the P Bar Ranch."

"Wonder what happened?" the other asked.

The cowboys rode on up to the front of the coach.

"Hey, Jacob," one of them called.

"Eb, Dusty," Jacob replied, as he slowed the horses.

"I see the Purvis brothers is belly down on them horses back there. What happened?"

"Henry here, kilt 'em," Jacob replied. "That's what happened."

"One man kilt all three of 'em? I mean, by hisself?"

"Yep. They made the mistake o' tryin' to hold up the stage while Henry was ridin' shotgun, only he didn't use no shotgun. He kilt all three of 'em with naught but a pistol."

"I'll be damn."

"You boys is well mounted. How 'bout ridin' on ahead 'n tellin' Sheriff Willingham what happened, would you? It might be he'd like to meet us 'fore we get to town," Jacob suggested.

"Sure 'nough, we'll do that for you," Dusty said.

HALF AN HOUR LATER, as they were approaching Tascosa, Sheriff Willingham met the stage, then rode alongside until they reached the depot.

By the time they arrived they were greeted by almost everyone in town, curious to see what had happened. Three young boys had run with the coach, keeping pace with it as it rolled down the entire length of Main Street.

"I'll take these boys off your hands," Sheriff Willingham offered, once the coach stopped, and taking the reins of the three outlaws' horses, he led them down to the undertaker's establishment.

Jesse Sheets was there as well and Ella rushed into his arms.

"Are you all right?" Jesse asked.

"Yes," Ella replied. "We're all fine, thanks to Mr. Brown."

By now tales of how Henry had stood alone against the three robbers had spread among all who were there to meet the coach.

"Mr. Brown," Jesse said, walking over to extend his hand. "I thank you for looking out for my wife, and to show my appreciation, you're welcome to eat at our place for free—that is for the rest of the month."

"Why, thank you, Mr. Sheets. I'll gladly accept that offer."

"Henry," a familiar voice said. "So, you are the Bellerophontes of the Texas Panhandle."

"I'm the what?" Henry asked, turning to greet Coop.

"Bellerophontes," Coop repeated, a wide smile on his face. "In Greek mythology he slew the three headed monster. Though in this case the three heads are on three different men."

Henry laughed. "Damn, Coop, if you don't come up with the damndest things to say."

"Come on down to the Equity Saloon, and let my buy you a sarsaparilla." Coop invited.

BY EARLY AFTERNOON SOL PRUFROCK, the undertaker, had all three bodies in open coffins, with the coffins standing up just outside his establishment. This not only appealed to the morbid curiosity of the town; it was also good advertising for his services.

There was a neatly printed sign posted above the three upright coffins.

THUS ALWAYS WITH BRIGANDS

Coop smiled at the sign which he thought was reminiscent of the words supposedly shouted by John Wilkes Booth, "Thus Always with Tyrants," though Booth did it in Latin.

"You goin' to write about this in our new paper, Mr. Cooper?" The question came from one of the men who had been drawn to the macabre viewing of the outlaw's bodies.

"I am indeed, Mr. Guthrie. "I am indeed," Coop replied.

COOP THOUGHT it was a fortuitous turn of events that allowed him to write a story in one of the earliest issues of the *Tascosa Pioneer* about his friend. Although this wasn't the first issue of the paper, it was the first issue since Walter Malone had returned to Ft. Worth.

Heroic Action of Shotgun Guard Saves Money Shipment

On the twelfth, instant, as the Dodge City and Tascosa stage coach was making its return from that Kansas town on the Arkansas, it was accosted by three armed men. The intention of the road agents was to relieve the stage coach driver of the thirty thousand dollars that was being transferred from the Dodge City Bank, to the Bank of Tascosa.

The outlaws were thwarted in their nefarious scheme by the intervention of Henry Brown, the shotgun guard who had but recently been hired to fill that position. In a demonstration of heroism, Mr. Brown, though outnumbered three to one, put his pistol into use, the balls thus energized taking fatal effect. The three men killed were the Purvis brothers, LeRoy and Gil, as well as Amon Hazel.

C. D. Montgomery, president of the Bank of Tascosa, has stated that had the money not arrived, every business in the city would have been put into serious financial jeopardy. "To that end not only the bank, but every citizen in town owes a debt of thanks to Mr. Brown."

The passengers of the coach, who by their very presence

could have been in danger, were most effusive in their thanks and praise for the courageous action of Mr. Brown.

"The Purvis brothers were once riders for my brand," One of the passengers, Mr. Chris Poindexter, an area rancher said. "I terminated their employment because of misdoings on their part and I've no doubt but that they would have extracted revenge had they known I was on the coach. I feel that I owe Mr. Brown my life."

THIS ISSUE of the *Tascosa Pioneer* was tremendously successful. Everyone in town had heard about the robbery but here was the story that they could read, and share, and it was in their own city newspaper. James Cooper and Henry Brown had arrived in town at the same time and now both were being feted by the townspeople, Henry for his heroism, and Coop for his words.

"YES, Mr. Brown is a hero, and he has my gratitude as well as my respect," C.D. Montgomery told the other businessmen at a luncheon they shared. "But that was a one-time thing. On the other hand what Mr. Cooper is giving us, by editing the newspaper, will have a lasting influence. It is my belief that a town doesn't really come into its own until it can boast of a newspaper. I have a feeling this will put us on par with every other city in Texas and will, without doubt, establish our position as the most important city in all the Panhandle, and throughout the state of Texas."

ALTHOUGH THERE HAD BEEN some excitement on Henry's first trip to Dodge City and back, the subsequent trips had been long, tiring, and downright boring. Within two trips he and Jacob had used up every old story they could tell, so that there were long periods when the only sounds were the clopping of the horses' hooves, and the squeaks and rattles of the coach body.

As the coach rolled into Tascosa it garnered a considerable amount of attention as its arrival always did. The stage coach, even more than the freight wagons, represented Tascosa's contact with the outside world. True, the freight wagons brought in more than a hundred thousand pounds of freight each month, but the coach brought passengers who provided a physical connection beyond the city, and it also brought mail.

As the coach rolled to a stop Henry climbed down, then stretched. He was growing tired of the long and tiring trips, and though he had enjoyed a few days of admiring recognition, that had worn off and now this was just another job—a monotonous job.

"Henry, Sheriff Willingham asked if you'd drop by and see him as soon as you got in town," Ernie Wallace said.

"Did he say what it's about?"

"No, he didn't. He just asked me to tell you to come see him."

"All right," Henry said. This request was met with some trepidation. As he walked to the sheriff's office, his mind played over all his past discretions that might have surfaced.

SHERIFF CAPE WILLINGHAM was a portly man with a jacket that pulled at the buttons. He was also nearly bald.

"You wanted to see me, Sheriff?"

"Yes, Henry, I did. I don't think I ever properly thanked you for what you did that day you saved the money shipment. Chris Poindexter swears you saved his life. And Jesse—he was awful happy to see his Ella get home safe."

"I was just doin' my job, Sheriff."

"Yes, and that's what I want to talk to you about."

"How's that?"

"You may have noticed that even though I'm sheriff, I never carry a gun. But I know I can only get away with that if there's somebody good with a gun to back me up." The sheriff started nodding his head. "Now, if you'd take the job, I'd like you to be my deputy. How does that sound to you?"

Henry was getting very tired of the long, exhausting stagecoach trips to Dodge City and back. He had no idea what the position of deputy paid, and he didn't ask. "Yes," he said. "I'm interested."

The sheriff smiled. "Somehow, I thought you would be, Mr. Brown."

"So, you have joined the commendable ranks of those notable men who ride upon the steed of justice to carry the fight against evil, have you?" Coop asked. He and Henry were dining at the North Star Restaurant.

"If you're asking me if I'm goin' to be Willingham's deputy, the answer is yes, I have."

Coop raised his glass, which in this case contained lemonade. "Then, as the *vox populi*, I say thank you."

Henry laughed, and shook his head. "You know, every now and then I can understand you, but it's getting to where most of the time I don't have an idea in hell what you're trying to say."

Visiting Drovers Proving to be Unwelcome Visitors

Residents of Tascosa cannot but notice an increase in the noise level and general uneasiness since a group of drovers under the leadership of Fred Leigh arrived. The drovers have brought a herd of cattle numbering some 1,100 to be fattened by the good grass that can be found south of the Canadian.

If the visits to our town by the men were for supplies and relaxation only, their presence would be welcome. But all too often such is not the case. These particular drovers, including their trail boss, are engaging in the pestiferous and most unwelcome sport of shooting at the moon and hurrahing the town. This indecorous activity has put everyone on edge, and the recommendation of this newspaper is that the good citizens of Tascosa do as little business with them as possible. Avoid the streets when they are in town and let them know in every way possible, that as long as they continue with their disruptive activity, they are not welcome in Tascosa.

IT WAS but two days after Henry took on the position as deputy that the drovers Coop wrote about, had come into town. Now they were making the rounds of the saloons in

Tascosa drinking heavily, shouting loudly, and becoming more and more belligerent.

"Henry, I'm worried about that bunch of drovers," Sheriff Willingham said. "I'm afraid they're going to cause some trouble if we don't stop them."

"What do you plan to do?"

"For now, all we need to do is keep an eye on them."

"All right," Henry agreed.

"HEY, FRED, DID YOU READ THIS?" a drover named James asked. Chuck James and Fred Leigh were standing at the bar in the Cattle Exchange.

"Did I read what?" Leigh replied.

"This here paper." James pointed to a newspaper lying on the bar.

Leigh chuckled. "I didn't come here to read no paper. I come here to drink."

"Maybe you should ought to read it," James said. "I mean, seein' as it's got your name 'n all."

"My name? What the hell's my name doin' in that paper?" Leigh asked as he reached for it.

At the moment, Coop was setting the type for one of the classified ads for the next issue.

Model Barber Shop and Tonsorial Parlor
Haircuts, Shaves, Shampoos
All in most approved way.
This Barbershop has been newly
Remodeled with finest appointments

JUST AS COOP finished setting the ad, two men came into the building.

"Yes, may I help you gentlemen?" Coop asked.

"Yeah, you sure can help us. My name's Fred Leigh, and you can stop printin' them lies about me 'n my men."

"I print only the truth," Coop said. "Have your men not been drunk and disorderly for the entire time you've been in our town? Have you not frightened and intimidated our citizens?"

HENRY WAS HALF a block away when he saw Leigh and another man go into the newspaper office. Henry had read Coop's article when the paper came out, so he was pretty sure that they weren't visiting Coop to tell him how much they liked it. He quickened his pace.

CHAPTER 15

"GENTLEMEN, I APPRECIATE YOUR INTEREST AND CONCERN," Coop said, "but I'm a very strong proponent of the first amendment to the Constitution of the United States."

"What?" Leigh asked, confused by Coop's words.

"Freedom of the press, Mr. Leigh. It means that as long as what I print is accurate, I have the right to print anything I wish, even though it might make some people uncomfortable." Coop's smile was condescending. "Actually, it is sometimes the job of the press to make people uncomfortable."

Leigh walked over to the cabinet that held all the type and put his hand on it.

"If I was to push this over 'n scatter all these little metal letters here that you use to make your newspaper, what would happen?" Leigh asked.

"You probably would be shot," Coop replied.

"And just how is it you're 'a plannin' on shootin' me, Mr. Newspaper Man?" Leigh asked. "You ain't even wearin' a gun."

"No, I'm not." Coop smiled, and pointed to Henry, who was standing behind the two men. "But he is."

"What the hell?" Leigh asked turning toward Henry.

"Get out of here now, and leave Mr. Cooper alone," Henry said as his hand rested over his pistol.

"Come on, Chuck, I think I need another drink," Leigh said.

With sullen expressions on their faces, the two men left the newspaper office.

"That was good timing," Coop said. "Thanks for dropping by."

Henry chuckled. "I read your article, and when I saw Leigh and his partner step in here, I was pretty sure it wasn't because they wanted to buy an advertisement. By the way, if you're going to print things that get people mad at you, it might be a good idea for you to start wearing your gun again."

Coop raised his eyebrows. "You might be right."

After Henry left and there was no further danger of being interrupted by belligerent cowboys, Coop started work on the article he was preparing for the next issue. He didn't bother to write it on paper, but composed it when he was setting the type. Once the story was set in the frame, he stepped back to read it, and though the type was backward, he had little trouble in comprehending it, for by now he was quite adapt at reading type in both directions.

Railroad For Tascosa

Whether the Southern Kansas will cross the Fort Worth and

Denver in Carson County, in Randall County, in Porter County, or in Oldham County is the question to which the people of the Panhandle are giving occasional thought. Otherwise, papers published in far away places, profess to have settled the question in favor of Carson, and in Carson the intersection may be; but how can our contemporaries know so much when the railway men themselves and their surveyors have not yet settled upon it? It is the announcement in some of the papers, that after the junction of the Southern Kansas with the Southern Kansas of Texas, then a line will diverge from that junction to Albuquerque, New Mexico, while others have just as confidently stated that it is to build straight to El Paso. Meanwhile, we are mindful of two things which we know to be facts: 1)that the charter of the two lines of the Southern Kansas both call for Oldham County, and 2) that a representative of the Southern Kansas of Texas said, distinctly, that at present no divergent line toward any other point but Tascosa is being contemplated.

AFTER RUNNING off the copies of the newspaper, Coop started toward the door to deliver them but he stopped and set the newspapers down. Remembering Henry's suggestion about wearing his pistol, he walked over to where the holstered pistol and belt hung on a wall hook, and taking it down, he strapped the gun on.

The weight of the gun at his side felt familiar and comfortable, and he loosened it before he started out.

AFTER DELIVERING HIS NEWSPAPERS, Coop stopped by the

Equity Saloon. Mickey McCormick, owner of one of the livery stables, and Temple Houston, one of the town's lawyers were sharing a table.

Temple Houston was well known in Texas because he was the son of the famous Sam Houston, the "Father of Texas." But Temple had managed to establish his own personality. He was a very flashy dresser and even in the Equity, he was wearing a big, white hat. He was considered a good lawyer but perhaps he was best known for his marksmanship, having won many a dollar participating in shooting contests all over the area.

"Coop, do you really think a railroad will come to Tascosa?" Mickey McCormick asked, pushing out a chair as an invitation for Coop to join them.

"Yes, Mack, I think it's very possible," Coop replied. "I mean, look at everything we have going for us. Tascosa has an abundance of water, two large mercantile houses, three lawyers, two blacksmith shops, a doctor, a drugstore, a dairy, a bakery, a school, and two liveries, including your own."

"Humph, what makes you think W.H. Woodman is a lawyer?" Houston asked. "I say he's an Englishman with a golden tongue who quotes Shakespeare more than he does Blackstone."

"But you must confess, Temple, that his Macbeth quotations do flow trippingly from the tongue," Coop said.

"Yes, well, methinks his talents are wasted in the court room. He should be on the stage," Temple said. Then, with a smile, he added, "The next one out of town."

Coop and McCormick laughed at his joke.

"You know, Coop, I'm not all that sure I want the railroad to come here," McCormick said.

"Why in the world would you say such a thing?"

"People rent horses and buckboards from me when they want to go somewhere. If the railroad came, they'd just ride the train, and I'd be out of business."

Coop chuckled. "Well, the tracks aren't going to go everywhere, and the more people there are, the better your business will be. On the other hand, if the railroad doesn't come here, people are going to start moving elsewhere. And then who would you gamble with?"

It wasn't a nonsensical question. Although Mack owned the livery stable, he derived much of his income from gambling, and had bought the livery from funds he had won at the tables. At one time, Mack had worked as a professional gambler having worked on riverboats and at several gaming houses before he settled in Tascosa.

"I guess I hadn't thought about that."

An attractive young woman, who worked as a dealer at the Equity, came over to the table and, standing behind Mack, let her hands hang loosely across his shoulders.

"Hello, Frenchie," Coop said. "What do you think about a railroad coming to town?"

"I know that Mack doesn't want the tracks to come, but I do," Frenchie said.

Frenchie had been given her nickname because she was from New Orleans and could speak French. Not much else was known about her because she never revealed much about her past. She told people that her name was Elizabeth, but even that may have been a subterfuge. Coop, who knew firsthand about changed names, respected her right of privacy.

"After listening to Coop, I've changed my mind," Mack said. "If the people left, who would play cards with us?"

"Thank you, Mr. Cooper, for putting some sense in my husband's head," Frenchie said. They had been married but a month earlier, though they had been living together for a long time.

"I am a member of the press, Madam, and it is my duty to enlighten, entertain, and educate all with whom I come in contact."

"Hey, Frenchie!" Jack Ryan called. "There's a card game making up." Ryan owned the Equity Saloon.

"I'd better get over there so the house can take some of their money," Frenchie said.

"I'll go see if I can get another game going," Mack said.

Shortly after Mack left a rather large woman, carrying three beers came to the table. This was Sally Martin, though because of her size, everyone called her Big Sal. Big Sal was in charge of the girls who worked at the Equity.

"Would a beer buy me a place at the table with you gentlemen?" Big Sal asked, putting one of the mugs in front of Coop, and the other in front of Houston.

"Why, Miss Sally, you're always welcome company, with or without a beer," Coop replied, greeting her with a friendly smile.

"I like you, Cooper, but now I've got a bone to pick," Big Sal said. "I think you ought to have stories in your newspaper that would be of more interest to women."

Coop had not expected this line of conversation with Big Sal. "All right, what do you have in mind?"

"I'd say there should be stories that a woman would want to read, like who's having who over for tea, or what books someone has read that they think is good. And sometime, you might put in an article about cooking or sewing or quilting or somethin' like that."

"You may have a point, at that. But right now, I don't have time to do it myself, and to be honest, the advertising isn't steady enough that I feel I could hire someone to work for me."

Sally smiled. "Well if you do find someone to write for you and it works out well, remember, I'm the one that gave you the idea."

"And a good idea it was, too," Coop replied with a little chuckle.

"Hold on there, Madam," Houston said, interrupting Coop. "Mr. Cooper is going to agree, but he will, no doubt, expect you to provide the stories for free, or at the very least, pay but a pittance for them. Don't sell your services too cheaply. You should have someone represent you in your negotiations with him."

"And would that be you, Temple?" Coop asked.

"That would be me."

"Oh, Mr. Houston, I could never afford to hire a lawyer."

"Not to worry, Madam. I shall do it pro bono. You won't owe me a penny."

"I think we can come to some mutually acceptable agreement," Coop said.

"You cheatin' son of a bitch!" a man shouted angrily.

Looking toward the disturbance, Coop saw a man standing over the table where Frenchie had gone to deal. Coop recognized him as Fred Leigh, one of the two men who had come into the newspaper office earlier in the day. At the moment, Leigh was holding a broken whiskey bottle. Across the table a man who was still seated, had streaks of blood streaming down his face, coming from a wound on his scalp. Frenchie and the remaining player in the game had backed away from the table so quickly that their own chairs were overturned, having been knocked down by their quick withdrawal.

"By god, nobody cheats me and gets away with it," Fred Leigh said, raising the broken bottle even higher.

"He wasn't cheating, you, Mr. Leigh," Frenchie said, in as calm a voice as she could muster.

"The hell he wasn't. I ain't won a single hand since this game started." Leigh put the bottle down and reached for the money that was piled up in the middle of the table. "I'm just goin' to take this pot to make up for it."

"That isn't your pot," the other player said.

Leigh chuckled. "Oh, yeah it is."

Big Sal had hurried over to the site of the disturbance. Taking the silk scarf from around her neck, she wet it in one of the whiskey glasses and used it to wipe away the blood on the face of the wounded man.

"Are you all right, sir?" she asked, solicitously.

"I . . . I'm not sure what happened. I'm a little woozy."

"If I ever catch you cheatin' me again, you'll be a hell of a lot more than a little woozy. You'll be a little dead." Leigh started to gather up the money and put it in his hat.

"Frenchie, did Leigh win that pot?" Big Sal asked as she continued to treat the wounded man.

"No, ma'm, he did not," Frenchie replied. "This hand hasn't been played out, yet, but Billy has three jacks showing and it looked like it might be his. That was when Mr. Leigh hit him."

Frenchie nodded toward the man Big Sal was treating, indicating that this was Billy.

"Mr. Leigh, I think you should go now," Big Sal said. "And leave the money on the table."

"Oh, I'm goin' all right. But I ain't leavin' this money on the table," the belligerent cowboy said. "I figure it's owed me."

"Frenchie says the money isn't yours," Big Sal said.

"You're takin' the word of a whore over me?"

"She's not a prostitute, but even if she were, I'd take her word over yours. Now, leave the money on the table and get out." Big Sal reached for Leigh's hat and he jerked it away from her, pushing her away from him so hard that the big woman fell to the floor.

Leigh moved to stand over her and pointing down at her, he snarled. "Look, you fat bitch. Stay out of things that don't concern you. I'm takin' this money, unless there's someone who thinks he can stop me,"

"That would be me," Coop said.

"What?" Leigh asked, looking over at Coop for the first time. "What do you mean, 'that would be me'?"

"I'm the one who's going stop you. You may disabuse yourself of any idea that you'll be taking any of this money, Leigh. Put it back on the table."

"What are you going to if I don't put it back? I know. You'll write another story about us ... baaad ... drovers." Leigh laughed at his own joke, and a few in the room nervously laughed with him.

"No, I've already done one story that you didn't like, so I don't think I'll write another one, but I'll tell you what I will do. If you don't put the money back, I'll kill you," Coop said easily.

Coop's calm, almost expressionless reply surprised Leigh, and the smile left his face.

Putting his hat full of money down on the card-table, Leigh raised his arm and pointed his finger at Coop. "My advice to you, mister, is to go back to your newspaper and write a story about the grasshoppers or somethin'."

A cold, humorless smile spread across Coop's face. "Mr. Leigh, you've just made a big mistake," he said in quiet, measured words.

"Oh yeah? And what would that be?"

"You're pointing your gun hand at me, but there's no gun in that hand."

"Don't you worry none about my gun," Leigh said confidently. "I can get to it fast enough if I need to." He started to drop his arm.

The smile left Coop's face. "No, leave your hand where it is."

"What?"

"Leave your arm pointing toward me," Leigh said. "If I see it so much as twitch, I'll blow your head off."

Leigh was caught between disbelief and fear. He was not used to anyone running a bluff on him, and he tried to laugh, though the laughter came out strained.

"What are you talking about? You don't even have a gun in your hand. Mister, you're crazy if you think I'm going to hold my arm out here like...."

Leigh started to drop his arm but in a lightning draw Coop had his pistol in his hand. The business end of the barrel loomed large in Leigh's face.

"No! Wait!" Leigh shouted. He put both arms up.

For the moment the loudest sound to be heard was the steady tick tock of the Regulator Clock which hung on the wall, opposite the bar. The customers were as shocked as Leigh by the Coop they were seeing now. They had come to know him as a gentlemanly mannered, well-spoken newspaper man. He could not have shocked them more if he had suddenly grown horns and a tail.

They observed the unfolding scene as intent on the proceedings as if they were the audience for a theatrical. In a sense, they were spectators in a theater, but in this case the scene being played out before them was much more intense than anything they had ever seen upon the stage. This was a drama of life or death.

Unable to control the sudden twitch that started in his left eye, Leigh examined the face of everyone in the room, hoping to see someone he could count on for help. But nobody offered to intercede for him.

Leigh looked back at Coop, realizing that he was on his own.

"Please, Mister," he said with a whimper. "What are you going to do?"

"Yes, Mister Cooper, what *are* you going to do?" Big Sal asked, having been helped to her feet by Mack and Frenchie.

"I think I'll just shoot him," Coop said, easily.

"No! My God! Please! No!" Leigh screamed.

"I'm tempted to tell you to go ahead," Big Sal said.

Leigh began shaking uncontrollably, and he wet his pants. "Miss Sal, please, don't let him kill me," he begged.

Big Sal sighed. "Get out of here, cowboy, and don't step foot in this place until you've learned to conduct yourself with civility."

"And while you're at it, wear dry pants," Frenchie

added, her comment drawing laughter from everyone else in the saloon.

"Y...yes ma'am," Leigh stammered. He reached for his hat, then pointedly, turned it upside down, dumping all the money onto the table before he turned to leave.

"I must say, Coop, I think you showed us a side of you that nobody's ever seen before. And here, I thought all you did was put out a newspaper," Temple Houston said.

"Publishing a newspaper is all I want to do," Coop replied.

CHAPTER 16

"YOU KNOW WHAT?" SHERIFF WILLINGHAM SAID WHEN Henry told him about the incidents, both in the newspaper office and at the Equity Saloon. "I think it might not be a bad idea if we had everyone leave their guns on the other side of the river. That goes for the drovers, and the local cowboys."

Henry chuckled.

"What's so funny?"

"I've done a lot of cowboyin', 'n I've visited a lot of trail towns, and I can tell you right now, they aren't going to like that."

"They don't have to like it, Henry; they just have to do it."

"We may as well get started then. I'll start in the Exchange Saloon," Henry said, hitching up his pistol belt as he left the sheriff's office.

When he stepped into the Cattle Exchange Saloon a few minutes later, there were five cowboys in the room. All five were armed.

"Men," Henry called out, "we've got a new law in Tascosa."

"What law is that?" one of the men asked."

"You can wear your guns anywhere you want, except in Tascosa. No guns allowed in town."

"Is that a fact?" one of the cowboys replied, belligerently. "Well Deputy, if you want my gun, you're goin' to have to take it from me."

"Do you have any kinfolk?" Henry asked. "Brothers, sisters, parents somewhere, maybe?"

"I got kinfolk. Why are you askin' such a fool question?"

"So I'll know where to send your gun after I take it off your dead body."

"Dewey, he's serious. I don't think we should be fightin' 'im on this," one of the other cowboys said.

"You're a good man," Henry replied. "Look, I don't want to have any trouble with you boys. Just park your guns somewhere on the other side of the river, then come on back and enjoy yourselves."

The men filed out of the saloon, leaving it empty.

"That's a hell of a thing, Deputy," the bartender said. "You just run off all my business."

"They'll be back, Jake. And when they come back you won't have to worry about getting the place shot up."

"Yeah," Jake agreed, "now that you mention it that would be a good thing."

Henry met no resistance in either of the other saloons so that by the time he was finished with his rounds, the town was gun-free.

Coop wrote about the new law in a subsequent issue of his paper.

Peaceful Nights

Since the implementation of Sheriff Willingham's new directive, that neither drover nor cowboy can come to town wearing their guns, Tascosa has enjoyed almost a full week of peace. There was, as might be expected, some opposition to the new law, but both Sheriff Willingham and Deputy Sheriff Brown have dedicated themselves to its enforcement.

If we are to secure rail service for Tascosa, then we must be able to provide for the railroad, and the new settlers the railroad would ultimately bring, a peaceful environment. We must face it, if we are to make our name known as a town where the sound of gunfire is greater than the sound of commerce, history will pass us by.

This newspaper applauds our sheriff for his move in eliminating guns from our community, and it asks the town's citizens to support the new law.

THE PEACE that Coop and the citizens of the town had welcomed, did not last. The event that set into motion the end of tranquility for Tascosa occurred on the day after Coop's article was published. It started when Fred Leigh, Chuck James, and six more of his men, approached the Canadian River that separated their herd from the town.

"This here's where we're supposed to leave our guns," Wilbur Sikes said.

"What's to keep someone from stealin' 'em?" Bo Murphy asked.

"Bo's right, Wilbur. If we leave our guns here, they might get stole," Tommy Albright said.

"Someone's goin' to have to stay with 'em," Murphy said.

"Who would that be, 'cause I sure as hell ain't goin' to be the one that does it," Albright said.

"We should 'a maybe left our guns back at the cow camp," Curley Marshal said.

"To hell with it," Leigh said, resolutely. "I ain't goin' back to camp to leave my guns there, 'n I ain't goin' to leave 'em here, neither."

"What are you goin' to do, then?" James asked. "Try 'n sneak 'em into town?"

""No, hell no, there won't be no sneakin' around about it. We're goin' into town with our guns in plain sight," Leigh said. "There's only the sheriff and his deputy," Leigh said, "and we all know the sheriff don't wear no gun, so that leaves one armed man against eight of us. This town depends on the business we give 'em, so I think it's time we let 'em know we can do any damn thing we want when we're here."

"Come on, boys, let's go!" Murphy shouted as he urged his horse into the river.

THE RIDERS WERE midway through town when suddenly Leigh held up his hand. "Stop! Stop, hold up!" he shouted.

The riders stopped, and Leigh pointed across the street to a woman who was obviously pregnant. She was feeding several ducks.

"I got a dollar that says I can shoot the head offen one o' them ducks," Leigh said.

"I got a dollar says you can't," James said.

"Anybody else want part of this?"

"I don't know," Curley Marshal said. "You sayin' you can do it with one shot?"

"That's what I'm sayin'."

"All right, I'll bet agin ya."

Leigh drew his pistol and took a long, slow, aim. The woman was paying attention to the task at hand, and she failed to notice that someone was pointing a gun in her direction.

Leigh pulled the trigger, and the sound of the gunshot was deafening. As he had bragged, he did shoot the head off one of the ducks, having chosen the one that was nearest the pregnant woman. Blood from the slain duck splashed up onto the woman's white apron and she fainted.

"Son of a bitch, Leigh! You killed her! What the hell did you do that for?" Murphy shouted.

"What? I didn't . . .," Leigh started to say but he was interrupted by a scream from one of the woman's neighbors.

"He killed Mrs. Foley!" The woman was pointing at Leigh, who was still holding a gun in his hand. "He killed Lucy!"

"Let's get out of here," one of the cowboys shouted, and everyone but Chuck James and Fred Leigh galloped away, leaving the two men in the middle of Spring Street. Leigh looked at the pistol in his hand, then put it away.

Sheriff Willingham, Henry Brown, and a Mexican man named Bustamante were standing behind the Howard and McMaster's Store when they heard the gunshot and the scream.

"How can there be shooting in town if nobody's supposed to have a gun?" Bustamante asked.

"That's a good question," Sheriff Willingham replied.

The three men moved to the front of the store to see what had happened. They saw the woman on the ground, splattered with blood, and they saw all the squawking ducks.

"It's Mrs. Foley and it looks like she's dead!" Henry said. "That son of a bitch killed her!"

Willingham rushed out into the street to confront the two drovers. "You sort of let your celebrating get away from you this time," he said as he held out his hand. "Leigh, you're under arrest for murder. You too, James. Hand over your guns."

"Are you crazy?" Leigh said. "Do you think I'm goin' to let some fat son of a bitch arrest me, just because he's wearin' a sheriff's badge? And I especially ain't goin' to let you arrest me for a murder which I didn't do, 'cause I didn't shoot nobody. What I shot was a duck which you would know if you'd take the time to have a look a' fore you come out here a' runnin' off at the mouth."

Willingham looked across the fence into the back yard, and saw the woman just beginning to sit up.

"Are you all right, Mrs. Foley?" He called.

"I think so," the woman answered in a strained voice. "I reckon I must've just passed out when that man shot my duck."

"See what I told you, Sheriff? I didn't shoot nobody," Leigh said.

"All that means is I won't be holdin' you for murder. But I'll still be takin' your guns."

"No, I don't think you will," Leigh said. "Me 'n my

friend James is goin' to have us a drink down at the Equity Saloon; then we'll be headin' across the river to where we got our cows bedded down. 'N I don't want to hear nothin' else from you."

In an act of defiance, Leigh and James rode down toward the Equity Saloon.

"You want me to go after 'em, Sheriff?" Henry asked.

"We'll both go after 'em," Willingham said. "They're goin' just where I want 'im to go. I've got a double barrel shotgun standin' in back of the Exchange Hotel."

Henry and the sheriff went down the street to the back of the hotel, which was next door to the Equity Saloon.

"I don't want no trouble in the bar, 'cause I don't want nobody to get hurt," Willingham said as he broke down the gun and checked the loads. He snapped it shut and the barrels closed with a click. "We'll just wait out front for 'em."

The two men walked around to the street and took up a position in front of the saloon. They didn't have to wait long before Leigh and James came out.

"I still can't get over that fat fool askin' me for my gun, 'n him not even bein' armed," Leigh was saying with a laugh."

"I'm armed now," Willingham said as he and Henry stepped out into the street. "And I'll be taking your guns if you please."

"Like hell you will!" Leigh shouted as he made a grab for his pistol.

Willingham pulled both triggers and there was a loud roar as Leigh's stomach and chest opened up.

Henry had left his pistol in the holster, believing that

no reasonable man would draw against someone who was holding a shotgun on them.

But Leigh and James had reacted beyond reason, and when Henry saw James going for his gun, Henry drew faster, shooting less than a second behind the roar of the double barrel twelve gauge shotgun. James went down as well, and though he didn't have gaping wounds with intestines lying on the ground, he was just as dead.

CHAPTER 17

JUDGE FRANK WILLIS HELD A HEARING TO DETERMINE WHAT should be done about the shooting of Leigh and James. The hearing, which was held in the Equity Saloon, was attended by drovers whose herds were nearby, including men from Fred Leigh's company. There were also several cowboys from neighboring ranches, as well as many citizens from within the town. All were in compliance with the no gun ordnance.

There were considerably more people than there were chairs to accommodate them, so seating capacity was increased by using several one-by-six boards stretched between the chairs.

In most of the trials and hearings Temple Houston acted as the prosecutor, but because Sheriff Cape Willingham and Deputy Henry Brown had specifically asked Temple Houston to defend them, W.H. Woodman was appointed to prosecute. C.B. Vivian, the district clerk, acted as bailiff.

"Hear ye, hear ye, hear ye, this hearing, in and for

Oldham County is now in session, the honorable Frank Willis, Judge presiding. Ever' body stand," Vivian shouted.

There was a scrape of boots and a rustle of skirts and petticoats as the gallery stood.

Judge Frank Willis was a portly man, bald headed, but with a full, gray, beard. He came into the court room with his black judicial robe sweeping out behind him. One of the saloon tables had been put into position to act as the "bench" and Willis sat behind it.

"You may sit," he said.

The scrape of boots and rustle of skirts was repeated.

Henry and Willingham were sitting at a table with Temple Houston, the table positioned up front and to the left side of "the bench." Woodman was at a table to the right side. Only two other tables were being used, one by Vivian who was acting as bailiff and the court clerk, and the other was used by Coop who would be covering the hearing for the newspaper.

"Attorneys for the defense and prosecution being present, Mr. Prosecutor, you may make your case," Judge Willis said.

Woodman was an Englishman who had been a barrister in his home country, and had passed the bar to practice law once he came to America. He had long blond hair and as he stood, he ran his hand through his hair, then tossed his head back, and began in a voice that would rival that of any actor upon the stage.

"I begin with the words of William Shakespeare. To thine own self be true, and it must follow, as the night the day, thou canst not then be false to any man."

Woodman paused to allow those words to be the most

recent conscious thought of everyone present. Then he continued.

"Those words are as true today as they were when the Great Bard penned them, lo some two hundred and eighty years ago." Woodman pointed toward Willingham and Henry.

"And I ask the two defendants here today if they . . ."

"Objection, Your Honor!" Temple shouted. "Sheriff Willingham and Deputy Brown are not *defendants* in a trial; they are *subjects* of this hearing."

"Objection sustained," Judge Willis said. "Mr. Prosecutor, you will not refer to them as defendants."

"Very well, Your Honor, I shall not refer to them so. But the terminology is not as important as the truth. And it is the truth that we seek. So, I ask the two . . . subjects . . . of this hearing, Sheriff Cape Willingham and Deputy, Henry Brown, to be true to themselves, and ask themselves, as this hearing is trying to ascertain, if it had been absolutely necessary for them to kill Mr. Fred Leigh and Mr. Charles James?

"It was well known that Fred Leigh had disdain for the ordnance that prohibited him from having a weapon and was both vocal and public in his disrespect for you. That raises the question as to whether your killing of him was more an act of hostility, than it was of self-defense as has been claimed.

"I suggest that, because Sheriff Willingham was holding a loaded shotgun, and Mr. Leigh's pistol was in his holster, that Sheriff Willingham had the advantage, and thus the plea of self-defense cannot be justified. And Sheriff Willingham's killing of Leigh, set in motion the gratuitous shooting by Deputy Brown, of Charles James. I am sure, Your Honor, that once you take all this into consideration, you will find for indictment and trial." Woodman sat down with an expression of confidence on his face.

Temple Houston stood, and for a long moment just stared at Woodman.

"Mr. Woodman, is it your contention that the shooting was not justified because Sheriff Willingham was holding a shotgun, whereas Leigh's pistol was still in its holster?"

"It is, sir."

"And is it your belief that because the pistol was still in the holster, that Leigh represented no danger to Sheriff Willingham?"

"That is correct."

"Your Honor, with the permission of the court, I would like to conduct a little experiment. I will be using two pistols, but before I begin, I will establish that there is no danger to the court by showing that the two pistols are empty."

"You may proceed," Judge Willis said.

Temple picked up two pistols, then handed both of them to the court clerk.

"Mr, Vivian, would you please ascertain for the court, that these weapons are not loaded?"

Vivian spun the cylinders on each of the weapons.

"They are both unloaded, Your Honor."

"What is the purpose of this experiment, Mr. Houston?" the judge asked.

"Allow me to demonstrate, and once the demonstration is complete, I will explain. Mr. Woodman, would you take this pistol please?"

Woodman took the proffered weapon, while Temple put the other pistol in his holster.

"Now, Mr. Woodman, I want you to point the pistol at me. When you see me start my draw, pull the trigger. But remember, don't pull the trigger until you see me begin my draw."

"What is the purpose of this? Of course if I already have the gun in my hand, I will be able to shoot you before you can complete your draw."

"Shall we try?"

Temple stood in front of Woodman then, drawing his gun in a flash he pulled the trigger. There were two clicks, as the hammer fell on empty chambers.

To those in the gallery, it was quite easy to see that Temple was able to draw his pistol, and pull the trigger before Woodman could. There was an audible gasp at the result.

"Your Honor, I object to this experiment," Woodman said. "Temple Houston has proven himself, on more than one occasion, to be much more proficient with a pistol than the average man. And because he was able to perform this trick against me, proves nothing."

"Perhaps if I expand the experiment," Temple suggested. He looked out into the gallery and saw some of the drovers who were with the same trail herd as had been Leigh.

"Who among you knew the two men, Leigh and James the best?"

"That would more 'n likely be Pauley," one of the drovers said, pointing to the man in question.

"You Honor, Defense calls Mr. Pauley . . ." Temple hesitated in mid- sentence and glanced toward the man.

"Lewis," the man said.

"Pauley Lewis to the witness stand."

"I don't know why you're wantin' me as a witness. I didn't see the shootin'," Pauley said.

"Please, Mr. Lewis, come to the front."

Not only Pauley, but the entire gallery was confused as to why he was being called as a witness when he didn't see the shooting.

Temple waited until the witness was sworn in before he addressed him. "Why did the others say that you knew Mr. Leigh and Mr. James the best?"

"I guess 'cause I come up here with Leigh 'n James last year."

"Would you say that the two were good friends of yours?"

"Oh, I reckon I could say as we was friends, but I wouldn't say we was particular good friends."

"Your Honor, where is counselor going with this?" Woodman asked.

Temple held up his hand. "I was merely establishing the relationship, I'll take this line of questioning no further, except to ask this. Mr. Lewis, was Mr. Leigh fast with a gun?"

"I'll say. He was about the fastest I ever seen. That is, 'till I seen you draw just now."

There was a ripple of laughter from the gallery.

"What about you? Are you fast?"

"Well, sir, I have to say that I am pretty good. But I'm not as good as Leigh was."

"You saw the experiment I conducted a moment ago, where I drew my pistol and pulled the trigger before Mr. Woodman pulled the trigger on his gun?"

"Yes, sir," Pauley said, as a big smile spread across his face. "That was some trick you done."

"Yes, it was. And now I would like to see you do it."

"What?"

"I want you to draw your gun and pull the trigger before Mr. Woodman can pull the trigger on his gun."

"I don't have no gun with me, seein' as we can't have no guns in town."

"You can use this gun. And as much as I am tempted, it will remain unloaded."

Several in the gallery laughed.

"All right, Mr. Woodman, the rules are the same as before. Don't pull the trigger until you see Mr. Lewis start his draw."

The two men squared off, then Pauley pulled his pistol, and just as Temple had done before him, he was able to draw and pull the trigger before Woodman could.

"I'll be damn!" Someone said, his words rising above the surprised reaction of the others.

"Thank you, you may sit down."

Temple waited until the young man was seated before he spoke again.

"Your Honor, Mr. Woodman, Mr. Lewis, ladies and gentlemen of the gallery, allow me to explain what you have just seen here.

"Approximately thirty years ago, a European named Franciscus Donders began studying something he called reaction time. Reaction time is how long it takes for you to act upon what you have seen. For example, if you see a vase turning over, your normal instinct is to try and catch it before it breaks. The time between when you see the vase about to fall, and before your hand *actually begins to move* in your attempt to grab it, is called reaction time.

"Mr. Donders also posited that the longest element of one's reaction is the time consumed while your brain is processing the information, and telling your arm to move.

"In the demonstration you just saw, Mr. Lewis had the advantage, because he had gone through the delay of reaction time. He had already processed what he had to do, and his brain had already told his hand to make the draw.

"Mr. Woodman, on the other hand, was unable to start that sequence until after he saw that Mr. Lewis had started his draw. That processing time delayed his response which meant that by time he told his finger to pull the trigger, it was already too late. Against anyone who is reasonably fast on the draw, our distinguished barrister, and almost everyone else, would lose every time."

Temple turned back toward the judge. "Your Honor, Fred Leigh had been ordered to disarm, but he chose not to do so. Now the prosecution's case is based upon the fact that the pistol was in the holster, while Sheriff Willingham was holding the gun. But I have proven by two demonstrations, that the very fact that the pistol was there, whether in the holster or not, represented a danger to Sheriff Willingham. Now in the case of Charles James and Henry Brown, it was just a matter of which of the two men had the fastest reaction time, and events proved that it was Mr. Brown.

"Given that Sheriff Willingham was acting in the line of duty, given that he had ordered the two men to disarm, and given that they did not, I would ask that you find this to be a case of carrying out their duties as officers of the law, resulting in justifiable homicide for each of them," Temple concluded as he walked to the table and sat down.

"Mr. Woodman, have you a rebuttal, sir?" Judge Willis asked.

Woodman, who had taken his seat after the demonstration, shook his head.

"I have no rebuttal, Your Honor. Prosecution rests."

CHAPTER 18

HENRY WAS MAKING HIS ROUNDS AND AS HE DID EVERY morning, he stopped by the newspaper office to share a cup of coffee with Coop. Coop normally greeted him with a smile and some sort of banter, but this morning he was quiet, and there was a forlorn look about him.

"Coop, what is it?"

"Walter Malone sent me some upsetting news this morning. The telegraph he got said this happened two weeks ago."

"What is it?"

"It'd be better if you read it yourself," Coop said, passing the printed sheet across his desk to Henry.

Death of Billy the Kid

"What?" Henry said, as soon as he read the headline of the story. "The Kid is dead?"

"That's what the article says."

Henry resumed reading.

Word has reached us of the events leading to the death of the infamous outlaw, William Bonney, sometimes known as Henry Antrim or William McCarty, but better known as Billy the Kid. The details are as follows:

On the night of July 14, Sheriff Pat Garrett and his two deputies approached abandoned Ft. Sumner, about 140 miles west of the town of Lincoln. The dusty old fort has been converted to living quarters. The residents were sympathetic to The Kid and the lawmen could extract little information. Garrett decided to seek out an old friend, Peter Maxwell, who might tell him The Kid's whereabouts. As chance would have it, The Kid stumbled right into the Sheriff's hands. Garrett has offered up his account of what happened.

"I had concluded to go and have a talk with Peter Maxwell, in whom I felt sure I could rely. We had ridden to within a short distance of Maxwell's grounds when we found a man in camp and stopped. To the great surprise of one of my deputies, he recognized in the camper an old friend and former partner he had known in Texas, a man named Jacobs.

We unsaddled here and entered an orchard which runs from this point down to a row of old buildings, some of them occupied by Mexicans, not more than sixty yards from Maxwell's house. We approached these houses cautiously, and when within earshot, heard the sound of voices conversing in Spanish. We concealed ourselves quickly and listened, but the distance was too great to hear words, or even distinguish voices. Soon a man arose from the ground, in full view, but too far away to recognize. He wore a wide-brimmed hat, a dark vest and pants, and was in his shirtsleeves. With a few words, which fell like a murmur on our ears, he went to the fence, jumped it, and walked down towards Maxwell's house.

Little as we then suspected it, this man was The Kid. We

learned, subsequently, that when he left his companions that night, he went to the house of a Mexican friend, pulled off his hat and boots, threw himself on a bed, and commenced reading a newspaper. He soon, however, hailed his friend, who was sleeping in the room, told him to get up and make some coffee, adding: 'Give me a butcher knife and I will go over to Pete's and get some beef; I'm hungry.' The Mexican arose, handed him the knife, and The Kid, hatless and in his stocking-feet, started to Maxwell's, which was but a few steps distant.

When The Kid, by me unrecognized, left the orchard, I motioned to my companions, and we cautiously retreated a short distance, and to avoid the persons whom we had heard at the houses, took another route, approaching Maxwell's house from the opposite direction. When we reached the porch in front of the building, I left Poe and McKinney at the end of the porch, about twenty feet from the door of Pete's room, and went in. It was near midnight and Pete was in bed. I walked to the head of the bed and sat down on it, beside him, near the pillow. I asked him as to the whereabouts of The Kid. He said that The Kid had certainly been about, but he did not know whether he had left or not. At that moment a man sprang quickly into the door, looking back, and called twice in Spanish, 'Who comes there?' No one replied and he came on in. He was bareheaded. From his step I could perceive he was either barefooted or in his stocking-feet. He was holding a revolver in his right hand and a butcher knife in his left.

Before he reached the bed, I whispered: 'Who is it, Pete?' but received no reply for a moment. It struck me that it might be Pete's brother-in-law, Manuel Abreu, who had seen Poe and McKinney, and wanted to know their business. The intruder came close to me, leaned both hands on the bed, his right hand almost touching my knee, and asked, in a low tone: 'Who are they Pete?' -at the same instant Maxwell whispered to me. 'That's him!' Simultaneously The Kid must have seen, or felt, the presence of a third person at the head of the bed. He raised quickly his pistol, a self-cocker, within a foot of my breast. Retreating rapidly across the room he cried: 'Quien es? Quien es?' 'Who's that? Who's that?' All this occurred in a moment. Quickly as possible I drew my revolver and fired, threw my body aside, and fired again. The second shot was useless; the Kid fell dead. He never spoke. A struggle or two, a little strangling sound as he gasped for breath, and The Kid was with his many victims."

HENRY PUT THE PAPER DOWN, and began shaking his head. "I can't believe it, that The Kid would be killed this way. I could see him being killed exchanging gunfire with a posse, or being ambushed someplace, but to be killed by one man, in the middle of the night?"

"Yes, Henry, but you and I both know this was bound to happen," Coop said. "If ever there was anyone destined to die young, it was Billy."

Henry nodded. "It's still hard to believe."

"This could just as easily been one of us. A few more stolen horses, a rustled herd of cattle now and then, or even a bank holdup. Somewhere along the line there would have been more killing."

"I know," Henry said. "I wonder what it was that made us leave Billy."

"You might say that we had an epiphany," Coop said. "We've left the outlaw trail to become responsible citizens. And I, for one, am glad that we made that decision before it was too late."

Henry stuck out his hand. "Let's make a vow between us, never to go down the outlaw trail again."

Coop took his hand. "Agreed," he said with a smile.

For the first several weeks after the hearing which had cleared Henry Brown and Cape Willingham, the ordnance against carrying guns in Tascosa had been strictly observed and as a result, the town enjoyed a period free of any gun violence. But when a big man, with broad shoulders and a narrow waist stepped into the Equity Saloon, Henry had a feeling that the situation was about to change.

The big man was wearing a tooled leather gun belt around his waist, with cartridge-bullet filled loops all the way around. His pistol, with a plain wooden grip, was holstered low and tied down on his right side. When he came into the saloon he moved to the side of the swinging bat wing doors and putting his back to the wall, perused the saloon.

"Look at 'im," Joe Krause said. "He's wearin' a gun. He must've missed the signs posted out on the road." Krause owned one of the two livery stables in town.

"No, he seen the signs all right. Look at the way he's wearin' his gun. He's come to town to dare anyone to take that gun away from 'im. Hell, he's lookin' for trouble," Mark Snider said. Snider owned the leather goods shop. "Deputy Brown's standin' up there at the bar. I wonder what's goin' to happen."

"I don't know, but I don't plan to be around when the bullets start flyin'." Krause said.

"Don't leave. Stick around for the show," Snider said. "But I'd advise you to get out of the way. You wouldn't want to be hit by one of those stray bullets now, would you?"

"No," Krause said. "No, I would not."

Krause got up from the table and walked away, but his morbid curiosity kept him from leaving. Instead, he chose a table in the farthest corner of the saloon, then sat there with his hands clasped on the table before him.

HENRY HAD SEEN the man come in, and at first he was willing to accept that the man was armed just because he was unaware of the ordnance. But there was something about the stranger that made Henry think he was aware of the ban on guns, but was deliberately defying it.

The man, pointedly, looked away when Henry glanced toward him, but it was obvious that the man had been studying him. Henry had the feeling that he was being measured as a target, but he didn't know why.

Henry had survived many gunfights over the years, not only because he could draw fast and shoot straight, but also because he had an innate sense about him, a gut instinct when someone was about to try to kill him. And he felt that now.

"Pete, do you have any idea who that man is?" Henry asked the bartender, speaking so quietly that only the bartender could hear him.

"Yeah, I've seen 'im before," Pete said. "His name is Chilton. I've never heard his first name."

Henry found the man in the mirror and, without being too obvious, kept his eye on him.

"Would you like another sarsaparilla?" Pete asked.

"Yes, thank you."

"What about Chilton? You goin' to tell 'im he can't wear his gun while he's in town?" Pete asked, as he put Henry's drink before him.

"That's my job," Henry replied, without too much enthusiasm. He tossed his drink down then turned toward Chilton.

"Mr. Chilton," he said.

Chilton smiled, an evil smile that showed tobacco-stained, crooked teeth.

"So, Deputy Brown, you know who I am, do you?"

"Mr. Chilton, I'm sure you must know that there are no guns allowed in Tascosa."

"Is that a fact?"

"Yes, it is, so if you're going to stay in town, I'm afraid I'm going to have to relieve you of your gun until you're ready to leave."

"What if I'm ready to leave right now?" Chilton asked.

"If that's so, then you can keep your gun."

Chilton touched the brim of his hat. "I'll be goin' then."

There was collective sigh of relief when Chilton left the saloon.

"Well, that's somethin'," Pete said. "I never would have thought someone like Chilton would give in so easy."

"Who is Chilton?"

"He fancies hisself a gun fighter, 'n truth to tell when I seen 'im come in, most especial the way he was eyein' you 'n all, I thought maybe he was goin' to call you out. He's just the kind that would like to brag to ever' one that he'd kilt a fast gun like Henry Brown."

Henry chuckled. "Well, I have to tell you, I'm glad he didn't."

"Want another drink?"

"No, I think I'll go over to the North Star and see what Jesse Sheets has cooked up for supper."

"You 'n him's got pretty tight, haven't you?"

"We have, but Jesse and Ella are easy to be friends with," Henry said. "They're nice people."

JESSE AND ELLA'S North Star Restaurant was a block east of the saloon on Main Street, and as soon as Henry stepped inside, he was greeted with a familiar and welcome aroma.

"Chicken and dumplin's," Henry said when he realized what was being served for supper. "I need to go get Coop; that's his favorite."

As Henry left to get Coop, Jesse walked out front with him.

"Tell him we have apple pie as well," Jesse said. "I know he likes that."

"I will, but believe me, with chicken and dumplin's he won't need anything else."

"Henry Brown! Draw!" Someone shouted from the growing shadows of the street. But even as the man shouted the challenge, he already had his gun in hand, and he pulled the trigger.

"Uhn!"

The grunt of pain came from Jesse Sheets who was standing beside Henry. In an instantaneous draw, Henry pulled his gun and returned fire.

The man in the street fired again, but this time, his pulling of the trigger was nothing but a reflexive action, muscle memory in the finger of a dead man. Chilton collapsed in the street as the sound of the three gunshots faded away without even an echo.

"No!" Ella screamed when she saw that her husband had been shot. She dropped to her knees beside him, sobbing uncontrollably.

Henry stood there, still holding the smoking gun in his hand, unable to offer Ella any comfort. And even if he had tried, the words would have come out hollow. Chilton was after him, not Jesse Sheets. Jesse had been shot down by accident, and it was all Henry's fault.

IT HAD RAINED EARLIER in the morning on the day of the funeral, and though the rain had stopped, the sky still hung heavy with clouds, as if heaven itself was in mourning. Coop, who had written Jesse Sheets obituary the day before, believed that this was the largest number of citizens he had ever seen gathered in Tascosa.

Tascosa had no church, nor did it have a resident minister. There was a Methodist circuit rider, the Reverend Joseph Bloodworth who came from time to time, as well as a Catholic Priest, Father Patrick Murphy. Because their visits were so infrequent, the citizens of the town would attend the services of whoever was there for them. As it so happened, Father Murphy was in town in time to conduct the funeral.

The last three people to have been buried in Tascosa's Boot Hill were outlaws. One of the three was Chilton, known only by his last name. He had been buried without clergy or ceremony. Ella Sheets had requested that Jesse not be lying next to outlaws, so his grave was dug as far from the others as possible.

Ella, dressed in black, stood next to the open grave. Because she had no family, three of her friends, Frenchy McCormick, Dolores Duran, and Emma Walker, also wearing black, stood with her.

It was quiet and still and Father Murphy stood there for a long moment as he looked out over the many gathered mourners. Then he began to speak.

"We gather here to commend our brother, Jesse Sheets, to God our Father and to commit his body to the earth. As Jesus Christ was raised from the dead, we too are called to follow Him through death to the glory where God will be all in all.

"O God, by whose mercy the faithful departed find rest, bless this grave,

and send your holy angel to watch over it.

"As we bury here the body of our brother Jesse, deliver his soul from every bond of sin, that he may rejoice in you with your saints forever. We ask this through Christ our Lord."

"Amen."

Father Murphy glanced toward the pall bearers Ella had chosen, six of the leading citizens of Tascosa: James Cooper, Henry Brown, Mickey McCormick, Ira Rinehart, Joe Krause, and Dan Cole. Then, using ropes, they lowered Jesse Sheets into his grave. When the coffin reached the bottom, the ropes were withdrawn and the six men stepped away. Father Murphy then nodded toward Ella who stepped up to the open grave and dropped a handful of dirt which, in the silence, could be heard falling upon the coffin.

"Ashes to ashes, dust to dust, in the sure and certain hope of eternal life," Father Murphy said.

THE FUNERAL RECEPTION was held in the North Star Restaurant which had been run by the Sheets from the earliest days of Tascosa.

"Will you keep the restaurant going?" Frenchy McCormick asked.

"I'm sure that's what Jesse would have wanted," she said, "so I intend to keep it open for as long as possible."

The reception was a somber affair, but for the duration, it united everyone in town in their support for the new widow, each person promising to make the North Star a regular eating place.

CHAPTER 19

Two Years Later

"You do know that there's no hope that the railroad will be coming through Tascosa," Coop commented.

"I know," Henry answered. "It's a shame."

The two men were having lunch at the North Star Restaurant.

"This town is dying, Henry. I've been told that John King and Ira Reinhart are both closing their stores. Professor Lawson is leaving and that means there won't be a school. Walter Malone has stepped aside from the newspaper He told me it's mine if I can keep it going, but advertising revenues are so low, I'm barely paying the bills."

"So are you goin' to try and make it work?"

Coop shook his head. "No," he said, sadly. "As much as I want to, I don't think I can. If the Fort Worth and Denver had lived up to its promise of bringing its tracks through here, the town would have survived. But there's no way Tascosa can survive without the railroad."

"Nobody can say you didn't try," Henry said. "I've read all the articles you've been writing about what a great opportunity it would be for the railroad and for the people, too."

"If you close down the newspaper, what will you do?" Henry asked.

"I don't know," Coop admitted. "The XIT is always hiring, but I just can't see myself as a working cowboy anymore."

"I can't see myself doing that, either. But if this town is dying, like you say it is, I'll be looking for a new job, too."

Within a few days after that conversation with Henry, Coop wrote the article that he didn't want to write.

Here, We Quit You

It is useless to make a long to-do about it, or to magnify a thing of no great moment, but this, kind friends, is the closing chapter in the history of The Tascosa Pioneer. From the beginning I have gone forth proclaiming to the world that we had here a country and a town of great worth. I have tooted our horn as faithfully as I knew how for the place in which I had hoped the paper would grow. I have kept the best foot forward and a smiling face under every condition; I have battled with difficulties and hoped against hope, but today I lay down the saber and give up the fight. The Pioneer is an institution of the past, a back number, a remembrance, and a dream.

It might have been different with The Pioneer, but it wasn't. Had Tascosa fared well at fortune's hands, that would have meant permanency for the newspaper. I do not criticize the town for failing to support my effort for indeed the citizens have been uniformly liberal in their support of it, and I acknowledge my deep debt of gratitude. But business has gone down to where profit is an unknown and an undiscoverable quantity, so the near future holds no promise. I ask which one of you would do aught but give it up at that? Sentiment is creditable and the home feeling may be hard to stifle, but after all is said and done, duty points to go wherever labor hath a sure reward.

So we quit to seek a new field, it would be childish to hesitate about it longer. We surrender the whole question; we feel that we have done all our duty, so we go now with a clear conscience, a heavy heart and a light pocketbook. To all my friends I say that you will be remembered for your friendship, and this time of pleasant association with place and people will never fade from memory. The warmest spot in my heart will long be for this little gem of a city on the turgid Canadian— sandy, sheltered, quaint, Tascosa.

No more will The Pioneer crack its ancient chestnuts in your tired ears; no more will it sing of the glory of our little town. We have had our say and now you can have yours, but as the pall of eternal silence settles down about us we are troubled with the thought: will anyone remember us when we are gone?

WHEN THE PRINT run was completed, Coop took all the

papers into the front of the building. It was telling that the first print run of the *Pioneer* had been 350 copies. This final print run was less than a hundred copies. He sat at the front desk and began to read through this, his last issue, when Henry Brown came into the room.

"Final edition?" Henry asked.

Coop nodded his head.

"Do you have any idea where you'll go now?"

"I'm afraid I haven't given it that much thought."

"You should go to Caldwell, Kansas," Henry said.

"Why would I want to go there?"

"Because I'm going there. I've been hired as their next City Marshal, and I want you to be my deputy."

"When do you plan to leave?"

"My position takes effect on July 3rd. I figure it'll take me at least ten days to get there, so I plan to leave here on about the twentieth of June or so."

"That's three weeks from now," Coop said. "Good, that'll give me time to do something with the press and all the printing accouterments."

"Why do you have to worry about it? This all belongs to Walter Malone, doesn't it?"

"When Malone offered to turn the paper over to me, I used what money I had left to buy the equipment from him."

"You put out a good newspaper, Coop. I was proud to tell people that the publisher of the *Tascosa Pioneer* was my friend."

"I appreciate the compliment and your offer of a job. As soon as I make arrangements for my equipment, I'll join you in this next chapter of our lives."

"I hadn't given any thought to how difficult it would

be for you to leave," Henry said. "It's easy for me; all I have to do is pack my clothes and my gun."

"Don't worry, I've got three weeks to get everything done. When you leave on the twentieth, I'll be riding right alongside."

CHAPTER 20

ALICE MAUDE LEVAGOOD WAS ONE OF 32 STUDENTS recently graduated from Park College in Parkville, Missouri. At the moment she was waiting at the railroad station along with another of the nine women who had just graduated.

"Why in the world would you even consider moving to Caldwell, Kansas," Mollie Dumont asked. "It is said to be a most frightful place."

"There's a school in Caldwell in need of a teacher," Maude said. "I am a teacher in need of a school. That seems to me to be a perfect match."

"But surely there are other schools that need teachers," Molly insisted.

"But are there other teachers who would agree to go to Caldwell? Or, do you think the town's reputation would frighten them away?"

"If they have any sense a respectable young woman ought to be frightened away," Molly said, trying to make a joke out of what was an earnest plea.

"I know you mean well, Molly, but I believe I was meant to go to this town," Maude insisted.

"The train is almost here," Molly said as she embraced her friend. "Please send me a letter to let me know what you're doing."

CALDWELL WAS a trail town in Kansas that was much more violent than Tascosa had been. Nothing was more indicative of its violence than the number of law officers who had been killed. George Flatt, a city marshal, was killed by a midnight ambush on Main Street. A few months later Assistant Marshal Frank Hunt was shot to death. Mayor Mike Meagher was killed in a street fight and after that City Marshal George Brown was killed when he tried to arrest a couple of troublemaking Texans. All this killing took place within a two year period.

Caldwell came by its wild reputation because of its location, sitting on the Chisholm Trail just north of the Oklahoma – Kansas border. It began its existence by building saloons and stores to cater to the randy tastes of the drovers who were herding cattle as far north as Wichita. Then, in 1880, the Atchison, Topeka & Santa Fe laid track into Caldwell, making it the terminus of the Chisholm Trail.

Quickly after the arrival of the railroad, more permanent structures were built, and ranchers and businessmen began to erect fine homes so that the city took on an aura of respectability. It soon became known as the "Border Queen" of Kansas.

This was the town in which Henry Brown and James

Cooper arrived after having spent nine days on the ride up from Tascosa.

"I know the prospect of a beer doesn't sound all that good to you, Henry, but I need something to get the dust out of my throat," Coop said, pointing to a building that advertised itself as the Red Light Saloon.

"I've got the same amount of dust in my mouth that you have," Henry said. "But a sarsaparilla will get rid of it just fine."

"All right, what do you say we go inside?"

The two men dismounted in front of the Red Light, looped their reins around the hitching rail, then stepped inside.

There were six men standing at the bar when Coop and Henry stepped up to order their drinks.

"How cool is your beer?" Coop asked the bartender.

"It's cooler than horse piss."

Coop laughed. "That's cool enough."

"And you sir?" the bartender asked Henry.

"I'll have a sarsaparilla."

"What?" the man standing closest to Henry said. "A grown man drinking sody pop? I tell you what, give this man a whisky, on me. Hell, I'm surprised he ever got weaned offen his mama's titty."

"Leave the man alone, Wheeler," the bartender said. "You got no call to be harassin' 'im like that.

Wheeler drew his pistol and pointed it at the bartender. "I said give the man a whiskey."

"You know, Mr. Wheeler, threatening someone with a gun is against the law. You will go to jail for that," Henry said, speaking in a voice that was as calm as if he were in a conversation about the weather.

"Ha! That ain't nothin' I got to worry about, on account of we ain't got no law in Caldwell. 'N seems like ever' time we do get a lawman, why, someone ups 'n shoots 'im."

"You have law now."

"Yeah? 'N who would that be?"

"Funny you would ask that," Henry said. "I am the law."

"You're the . . ."

That was as far Wheeler got in his response because suddenly, and moving so fast that it took everyone by surprise, Henry pulled his pistol and brought it down, hard on Wheeler's head. Wheeler dropped his pistol as he collapsed, and Coop quickly grabbed the gun.

"Mister, you ought not to have done that," one of the other drinkers at the bar said. "Ben Wheeler ain't somebody you want to get on his bad side."

"By saying that, are you implying that Mr. Wheeler actually has a good side?" Coop asked.

Coop's question was met with nervous laughter.

"Where might I find the mayor of this town?" Cooper asked the bartender. "After I put Mr. Wheeler in jail, I'll need to be sworn in so that it'll be legal to keep this man in jail."

"Sworn in?" the bartender asked. "You mean you really are a lawman?"

Henry smiled and extended his hand across the bar. "The name is Henry Newton Brown, soon to be City Marshal. And this is James Cooper, the man who'll be my deputy."

The bartender smiled. "My name's Wash Walker. Welcome to Caldwell, Marshal."

"The mayor?" Henry asked again.

"The mayor, yes. You'll find him at the city hall. Go down here to Main, turn left and go one block. The City Hall, the mayor's office, and the jail are all together on the corner of Fourth and Main."

Coop helped Wheeler to his feet.

"Mr. Wheeler, I really don't want to start my first day as City Marshal by putting someone in jail," Henry said. "If you promise to let me drink my sarsaparilla in peace, I'll let you go."

With a sheepish grin, Wheeler took out a nickel and laid it on the bar. "Wash, this here's for the marshal's sody pop."

A FEW MINUTES LATER, Henry and Coop were standing in front of A.N. Colson, the mayor of Caldwell. Colson was a small, thin man with a prominent Adam's apple, thin white hair, and pale blue eyes enlarged by thick lenses in a pair of wire-rimmed glasses.

"Mayor, I'm Henry Brown, you sent me this letter offering me the job as City Marshal," Henry said, holding out the missive.

"Yes, I did," Mayor Colson said. "And who is this gentleman?"

"James Cooper, Mr. Mayor," Coop said, holding out his hand. "Henry has asked me to be his deputy."

Colson smiled. "Good, good, it will be nice to have a new marshal and a new deputy. I feel safer already."

It took but a few minutes for Henry and Coop to be sworn in as marshal and deputy marshal.

"Tell me a little about the town," Henry said.

"Well, sir, at the last census we had a population of

about 2000 folks, though I expect it's a little bigger than that now," Mayor Colson said. "We have two banks, two churches, two newspapers, two doctors, four lawyers, an opera house, three hotels, a roundhouse and stock yards down at the depot, a two story brick school house, two livery stables, half a dozen restaurants, about two dozen businesses, too many to mention here, and of course, the saloons."

"We stopped at one of them," Henry said. "The Red Light, I believe it was called."

"Yes, well, they call it a dance house and I reckon you know what that means. It's run by George and Maggie Woods, and while they have never given us any trouble, quite often their clientele certainly does. We have a dozen more saloons, but we have more trouble from that saloon than we do from all the others combined. Of course, they have more women at the Red Light than the rest of them combined. But from what I've heard about you in Tascosa, I'm sure you'll have no trouble maintaining peace and order."

"Oh, I'm quite sure my deputy and I will be equal to the challenge," Henry said.

"Now, as to your compensation, we'll be able to pay you a hundred dollars a month. And you, Mr. Cooper, will draw seventy-five dollars a month."

"That's very generous!" Henry said. "My last job only paid sixty dollars a month."

"I thought you'd be pleased," Colson said. "What about you, Mr. Cooper? I expect this is more than you were paid at your last job too."

Coop chuckled. "When you consider that my last job

didn't pay anything at all for the last six months, I would say, yes, this is paying more."

The mayor looked surprised at Coop's response. "What kind of job did you have that paid nothing?"

"I published a newspaper in a dying town," Coop said.

"Ah, well, yes, I suppose I can understand that. But, that's not a problem for our local newspapers; we have two of them, and both of them are doing very well, I'm happy to say."

"That's very good," Coop said. "I may be prejudiced, but it is my belief that a healthy newspaper is the backbone of a healthy community."

"I agree," Colson said.

"We'll need to find a place to live," Henry said.

"The Southwestern Hotel is next door to us. It's that way," Colson said pointing. "The Leland Hotel is also next door but it's the other way." The Mayor pointed in the opposite direction. "The Southwestern is a fine hotel and that's where the two of you will be staying. The city will pay for your rooms, but we don't pay for your food. You'll be responsible for your own meals."

"That won't be a problem," Henry said. "I'm pleased that you're offering quarters beyond that of sleeping in a jail cell."

"Yes, well, it hasn't always been so. But, in order to insure ourselves that we could get a marshal worth his salt, I got the city council to agree to pay for the rooms.

"Your office and the jail are downstairs, Marshal. The city is now in your hands."

As HENRY and Coop were visiting with Mayor Colson

some three blocks east of them, a train was arriving at the depot. Maude Levagood looked through the window to try and get an idea of what this town, into which she had cast her immediate future, was like. From the wild tales she had heard about Caldwell, she half expected to see nothing but ramshackle buildings and tents. She was pleasantly surprised to see a neighborhood of neat painted houses with well- tended lawns. Also, many of the business buildings were of stone or brick construction. The appearance of the town relieved some of her anxiety.

"Caldwell! This is Caldwell!" the conductor was calling as he walked swiftly through the car.

The train rumbled to a stop, then Maude stood and moved to the end of the car. When she stepped down, there were three women carefully studying the arriving passengers. When it became evident that Maude was the only unaccompanied female to detrain, the three women came toward her.

"Would you be Miss Levagood?" one asked. The questioner was a stout woman who was wearing a rather plain dress that only added to her matronly looks.

"Yes, I am."

The woman smiled.

"I'm Emma Rittenhouse of the Ladies Auxiliary School Board, and this is Letty Fleming and Cora McKinney."

"We're so happy to have you come," Cora said.

"I'm pleased to have arrived," Maude said.

"Oh my poor dear, you have to be exhausted," Emma said, "but we are all so excited to have a school teacher, we've forgotten our manners. I know you want to know where you will be living."

Maude smiled. "I would like to rest for a minute."

"We'll take you to the Southwestern Hotel where the school has a room reserved for you," Letty said. "Then after a while, we'll take you for a tour of the school. I think you'll be quite pleased; I know we're proud of it. Then, tonight, the LASB will host a dinner in your honor."

"Thank you," Maude said. "It was very nice of you ladies to meet me."

"Come, we'll make arrangements for your luggage to be delivered to you at your room in the Hotel," Mrs. Rittenhouse said.

HENRY AND COOP were standing at the desk of the Southwestern Hotel.

"Your rooms will be on the third floor, 302 and 303, right across the hall from each other."

"Do they overlook Main Street?" Henry asked.

"Room 302 overlooks Third Street."

"I would like a room overlooking Main Street," Henry said.

"I'm sorry, Marshal, but these are the rooms that the city has reserved for you."

"All right, Third Street it will be, then."

As the clerk continued with the process of checking them in, four women entered the hotel. Henry thought one of the women, the youngest of the group, was exceptionally pretty. She had light brown hair, bright blue eyes, high cheek bones, and full lips. She was a very slender woman, though not so slender as to hide her curves.

"Mr. Deckert, this is Miss Levagood, our new school teacher," one of the four women said. "She will require a room." The woman spoke with the authority of someone who was used to being heard.

"I'll get right on it, Mrs. Rittenhouse," the desk clerk replied, "as soon as I finish checking in these gentlemen."

"Didn't you hear what I said? Miss Levagood is our new school teacher, and as we have a full day planned for her; we can't waste time getting her checked in to your hotel. The school board maintains rooms here, but if you can't respond quickly enough, we can always move our business to the Leland Hotel."

"Mr. Deckert, please attend to the lady," Henry said. "My deputy and I can wait." Henry smiled at Maude, and touched the brim of his hat.

"Thank you Mister, uh . . ." Mrs. Rittenhouse said.

"Brown. Henry Brown," he said, not taking his eyes from Maude. "Marshal Henry Brown."

SEVERAL MINUTES LATER, after Henry and Coop were both checked in, they went to lunch in the hotel dining room.

"She's a very pretty woman, isn't she?" Coop asked.

"Who's a very pretty woman?"

"Mrs. Rittenhouse."

"What!" Henry said so loud that a few of the other diners glanced toward him.

Coop fought hard to control his laughter.

"Well, you were making cow eyes at one of them. I just wasn't sure which one it was."

Now, Henry laughed as well.

"Yes," he said. "Miss Levagood is an attractive woman."

CHAPTER 21

IT DIDN'T TAKE LONG FOR HENRY AND COOP TO BE TESTED. It was not quite two weeks after they arrived when Coop stepped out of the marshal's office and saw four men riding up Main Street. They stopped in front of the bank, which was just across the street from the city hall and next door to the opera house.

Stopping at the bank would not, by itself, be so notice-able. But it was what happened next that caught Coop's attention. Three of the men dismounted and handed the reins of their horses to the fourth man, who remained mounted.

Coop stepped back into the marshal's office.

"Henry, you might want to have a look at this."

When Henry stepped outside Coop told him what he had seen. "They weren't wearing masks or anything, but there was something about the way they were acting that got my attention."

"Well, what do you say we go on down to the bank and see what's going on?" Henry suggested.

They hadn't gotten half way there when they saw three

men come out of the bank. All three were carrying pistols and one was carrying a bag.

"You men!" Henry called. "Stop where you are! I want to talk to you!"

"It's the law!" one of the three men said.

"Shoot 'em, shoot 'em!" another yelled.

The three men began shooting, and Coop could hear the bullets as they whizzed by, some so close he could feel the wind of their passing.

Coop and Henry did not have their guns in hand when Henry first issued the challenge, but both drew their guns and returned fire.

Coop's first target was the man carrying the bag, and he was hit and went down. One of the other men grabbed for the bag.

"We ain't got time for that! We gotta get out of here!"

"We come for the money, 'n I ain't a' leavin' it!"

The one who had been mounted dropped the reins of the other three horses, then spurring the sides of his horse, urged him into a gallop. When he dropped the reins the other three horses, now startled by the gun fire, ran away.

"Eddleman, you yellow-bellied son of a bitch!" One of the two remaining men shouted.

By now Coop and Henry were standing in the middle of Main Street as Eddleman galloped toward them. At that very moment Coop saw a young boy who had been standing in front of Horner's Drug Store step out into the street.

"No, kid, get back!" Coop shouted.

The boy was either too frightened or too mesmerized by what was going on to respond to Coop's warning, so

Coop dropped his gun and dashed out in front of the approaching rider. Scooping the boy up, he dived for the ground and, holding the boy, rolled out of the way just as the horse came thundering by. The flashing hooves of the horse missed them, but they were peppered with the dirt clods the horse had kicked up.

Henry fired at the retreating Eddleman, knocking him from the saddle. Leaving the boy, Coop ran back to pick up his pistol, but the gun was no longer needed. Three men lay in the dirt in front of the bank and the fourth, the man the others had called Eddlemn, lay in the middle of the street about twenty yards away.

A woman rushed out of the drug store and grabbed the little boy who was just now getting up. The town was quiet for a long moment, then first one, and then another of the citizens began to reappear.

"Damn me if I ain't never seen nothin' like that!" someone said.

"That new marshal. He's pure dee somethin', ain't he?"

Townspeople began to gather around the three men who lay dead in front of the bank. One of the dead robbers was still clutching the money bag.

"Sir?" a woman's voice said, and Coop turned toward it.

"Yes, ma'am?"

"You saved my son's life," the woman said. "Bless you. God bless you. Thank you. Thank you so much."

"I'm just glad I was in the right place at the right time," Coop said.

LATER THAT SAME DAY, Coop and Henry were having a

drink in the Exchange Saloon. The Exchange Saloon was the first building a traveler would encounter when coming into town from Oklahoma, and because of that it had a sign, pointing south, which read, "First Chance." That was because alcoholic beverages were against the law in "The Nations" and this would be the first opportunity any traveler would have to buy liquor. Going south, the other side of the sign read "Last Chance" for the same reason.

Sharing the table with them was Tell Walton, who was the editor and publisher of the *Caldwell Post.*

"The four dead bank robbers are Jim Talbot, Bob Munson, Doug Hill, and Dick Eddleman," Walton said. "What I can't understand is why they came back into Caldwell. They had to know they'd be recognized. I wonder why they didn't wear masks."

"Why do you say they'd be recognized?" Henry asked.

"You know Mayor Meagher and Marshal Brown were both murdered, don't you?" Walton asked. "By the way, Marshal Brown wasn't any kin to you, was he?"

"No, George Brown and I weren't related, and yes I know that he and the mayor were murdered, but what does that have to do with the bank robbers?"

"It has everything to do with it. They're the ones who killed the mayor and the marshal."

"I didn't know that. I can see why you say they were foolish to try and hold up a bank here," Coop said.

"Not just here," Henry said. "Anyone who'd try and hold up a bank anywhere is a damn fool. If you're going to ride the outlaw trail, there are a lot easier ways of doing it than holding up a bank. Look at Jesse James. He's probably the most successful bank robber ever, but look what happened to him and his gang when he tried to hold up that bank in Minnesota. It was a total disaster and he was lucky to get out of alive."

Coop chuckled. "So you're saying you don't have plans to ever rob a bank."

Henry laughed as well. "Well, if I ever did decide to hold up a bank, I sure wouldn't do it in the same town where everyone knows me."

"Say, Coop, I wrote up the story about the bank robbery to go in the next issue of the *Post*," Walton said. "I wonder if you'd take a look at it for me. I'd like to know what you think about it."

"Sure, Tell, I'd be glad to," Coop replied. "But why me?"

"I'd value your opinion, because I know you published a newspaper down in Texas, didn't you?"

"Yes, but if you know about that, you also know that my newspaper went broke."

"The whole town went broke," Tell said. "You can't publish a newspaper if there's no town to support it."

"You're right about that," Coop said. "I'll stop by your shop later."

"How about coming with me now? I've got the story set, but being an old newspaper man, I expect you can read it backward as well as forward."

Coop followed Tell to the office of the *Post*, and there, stood at the composing table to read the story.

"It's a good story, Tell," Coop said after a couple of minutes, "but you've sort of overplayed my role in it. Marshal Brown got three of the robbers."

"I doubt that Mrs. Kirby thinks I've overplayed your role."

"Mrs. Kirby?"

"She's Bobby's mother. The little boy you saved."

"I'm just glad I got to him in time."

"Tell me, Coop, how much do you know about Marshal Brown?"

"What do you mean?"

"It's just that I've heard stories about his past, rather disturbing stories, I might add. It is said that he is deadly fast on the draw, accurate when he shoots, and is someone who is prone to shoot at the slightest provocation."

"He is fast and accurate. But the suggestion that he would shoot without provocation is false. I know a great deal about him. He's my friend, and I believe I can say without equivocation, that he's my best friend. I wouldn't take kindly to anyone spreading untrue rumors about him."

"Oh, please don't get me wrong, Coop. I wasn't spreading false information; I was coming to you for accurate information."

"Now you have it," Coop said.

"Why don't you come work for me?" Tell asked.

"What?"

"As my editor. Currently, I'm both publisher and editor. I really think my paper would be better served if I just retained the title of publisher, and let someone else be the editor. Someone like you, who has both the experience and the skill to do the job. I'm quite sure I can pay you as much as you're getting now."

"I appreciate the offer, Tell, I truly do. But if I ever get back into the newspaper business again, I'll need to be top dog. I'm sure that an old newspaper man like you can well understand that."

Tell nodded. "As a matter of fact, I do. I'd love to have you working for me, but I fully understand your position."

"On the other hand, if you ever plan to sell out, come see me first. I'd like the chance to try and raise enough money to buy it."

"I don't see that in my future, but I've heard some stories about *The Index*, over in Medicine Lodge."

"Oh? What have you heard?"

"*The Index* is owned by Wylie Payne. Payne also owns a mercantile and the bank. The bank takes up most of his time, and he's beginning to let the newspaper slip. I think he'd be willing to sell it if he could find a buyer."

Coop got a pensive look on his face. "Thanks for the information, Tell. Maybe I'll look into it."

THAT EVENING, Henry had dinner in the Peacock Restaurant with Maude Levagood. Henry dressed for the occasion complete with a jacket and string tie. Maude had also made an effort to look her best, abandoning the modest dress of a schoolmarm for the more attractive, even provocative scoop neck that showed her neck and chest, all the way to the top of her breasts.

"Miss Levagood, I appreciate your agreeing to have dinner with me this evening," Henry said.

"And yet you call me 'Miss Levagood'. That's what my students call me."

"Well, I wouldn't want to be so bold."

"Heavens, Henry," Maude spoke the name almost as if her tongue was caressing the word. "Have you ever thought that perhaps I might want you to be so bold?"

A huge smile spread across Henry's face. "Well then, in that case I'll be happy to call you Maude."

"You do know that you're the talk of the town, don't you? Everyone's calling you a hero, the way you single-handedly stopped the bank from being robbed."

"It wasn't single-handed by a long shot," Henry said. "My deputy was with me. And if there was a hero, it would be Coop, and the way he saved that little boy who wandered into the street."

"Yes, that was a wonderful thing, all right. But Coop could have done that even if all Bobby had done was run out in front of a runaway wagon," Maude said as she put her hand on Henry's. "No sir, the real hero is the one who stood up to the bank robbers and saved the money for the whole town."

Henry was uncomfortable with the praise Maude was bestowing upon him. He cleared his throat and looked away.

"Say, would you attend a play with me?" he asked changing the subject. "A touring group is arriving today to present *The Mulligan Guard Picnic*. Coop knows about these things and he says it will be a good show."

"That all depends," Maude replied.

"Depends on what?"

Maude leaned across the table and as she did, her dress fell forward slightly disclosing a little more of the tops of her breasts.

"It depends on whether you are asking me to accompany you and Deputy Cooper, or if the invitation is for me alone."

Henry read her meaning. "Why, it's for you to accompany me, alone."

"In that case, I'd be very happy to attend the play with you."

———

THE CALDWELL HOUSE was on the corner of Main and Seventh, and there was a significant crowd gathered in front of the theater, waiting for the box office to open.

"There's the marshal folks!" someone shouted when Henry and Maude arrived, having walked from the hotel. "He saved the town when he stopped that bank robbery. If Talbot and his gang would 'a got away with our money, purt nigh the whole town would 'a gone broke."

Several added their own affirmative comments and congratulations, and they expressed their appreciation by inviting Henry and Maude to the head of the line.

"See," Maude said quietly as they walked down to the front row seats in the as yet empty theater. "You really *are* a hero."

The play was a musical comedy enjoyed by all.

In their variety act the actors, Harrigan and Hart, were wearing exaggerated military uniforms, though they represented no known army. Harrigan was the smaller of the two actors, and his uniform was much too large for him. Hart was significantly larger, and his uniform was so tight that the jacket wouldn't close.

The uniforms alone drew laughter from the audience as they asked each other the obvious question: why didn't the actors just change uniforms?

They began marching around the stage as if in some sort of military drill, though they were making many missteps and a few times almost dropped the rifles they were carrying. And, as with the uniforms, Harrigan was carrying a very long rifle, while the rifle Hart was carrying was so small as to almost be lost. As they paraded around on the stage, they sang a marching song.

We shouldered arms
And marched
And marched away,
From Baxter Street
We marched to Avenue A.
With drums and fifes
How sweetly they did play
As we marched, marched, marched
In the Mulligan Guards.

Later in the play there was a humorous exchange between Harrigan and Hart.

"You stole a penny," Hart scolded. "Why, do you know it is as much a sin to steal a penny as it is to steal a dollar? Now, how do you feel?"

"I feel like a chump," Harrigan said. "There was a dollar lying next to the penny."

The audience laughed uproariously at the joke.

After the play Henry walked Maude to the Southwestern Hotel, her home being a room on the same floor as his own.

"You may kiss me goodnight, Henry," Maude said with pursed lips.

Henry kissed her, then he walked downstairs feeling as if his feet weren't touching the ground as he hurried next door to the marshal's office. Coop was there reading by the light of a kerosene lantern.

"Did you enjoy the play?" Coop asked.

"Very much." Henry could barely contain his excitement.

"I thought you might. It has played very well all over the country."

"You know who went with me to the play?" Henry asked.

"I would guess Miss Levagood."

"No."

"No?" Coop asked. "Then who did go with you?"

"I went with the future Mrs. Henry Newton Brown."

CHAPTER 22

COOP WAS AT THE *CALDWELL POST* VISITING WITH THE publisher.

"I thought you sold your printing press to the *Wilson County Courier*. Didn't the sale go through?" Tell Walton asked.

Coop shook his head. "No, when it came time for them to pony up the money, they didn't have it. That's the third time I've thought I had it sold, and it fell through."

"Well, there *is* a limited market for selling a printing press," Tell said. "It's not like trying to sell a horse or a buckboard."

"So I have discovered. Tell, I hate to ask you . . ."

Tell held up his hand before Coop could even finish the question.

"I wish I could buy it from you, but to be honest I can't afford it either. You used to own a newspaper; you know how hard it is to make any money in this business."

Coop laughed. "Oh, yes, I know how it is all right. But I wasn't going to ask you to buy it; I was just going to ask you to store it for me for a little while longer. It's not something I can keep in the hotel."

"Oh, well, if that's all you want, sure. That press isn't causing me any trouble and it can sit right where it is."

"Thanks."

"But just out of curiosity, what are you going to do with it?" Tell asked.

"Right now, I don't have the slightest idea."

ABOUT A MONTH after Coop's conversation with Tell Walton, Rudy Draper, who was one of the owners of the York, Parker, and Draper Mercantile, asked Coop to bring Henry to the store.

"But don't tell him why you're bringing him here," Draper said.

"I can hardly tell him anything when I don't know what's going on," Coop replied.

"It's good that you don't know; that way you can't tell him. Give him any excuse you need, but get him into the store at two o'clock."

"All right," Coop agreed.

When Coop stepped into the marshal's office a short time later he saw Henry cleaning one of his pistols.

"Is the town quiet?" Henry asked.

"It appears to be so. By the way, Rudy Draper wants you to be at his store at two o'clock."

Henry looked up in surprise. "Why?"

"That, I can't tell you."

"What do you mean, you can't tell me?"

"I can't tell you, because I don't have an idea in hell what this is about."

"Damn, I hope we aren't in some sort of trouble. You aren't aware of anything, are you?"

"No. As far as I know everyone in town has been pleased with the job we're doing. I don't expect it's anything like that."

"I hope they aren't planning to lower our salaries. Heck, we've brought more money into the city through fines, than they pay us."

"That's true," Coop said. "But it seems like towns are always in trouble for money. And they do pay us more than most marshals' get. Hell, I'm just the deputy, and they pay *me* more than most marshals' get."

"This is not a good time for me to have my salary cut. I have plans," Henry said.

"What kind of plans?"

"Plans like maybe getting married."

Coop smiled. "That's great, Henry! When are you and Maude going to tie the knot?"

"I don't know."

"You mean you haven't set the date?"

"I mean I haven't asked her to marry me yet."

AT TWO O'CLOCK that afternoon a worried Henry Brown, accompanied by an equally concerned James Cooper, stepped into the largest store in the city. Henry was surprised to see a rather substantial crowd there, including most of the business men and women of the city. Mayor Colson was there as well.

Frank Jones, who was president of the Caldwell Business Association, stepped forward and held up his hands to call for attention.

"What the hell, Frank, are you going to make a speech or something?" someone asked.

"Quiet, let 'im talk. This is important," someone else said.

Jones began to speak.

"Marshal Brown, before you arrived in Caldwell, we had the reputation of being one of the wildest towns in Kansas. Drovers and cowboys paid little attention to decorum, and no attention at all to our laws. Our saloons yes, even our businesses, became dens of iniquity, for no one could still the willingness to fire a gun in drunken celebration, or even worse, resort to gunplay to effect a permanent settlement to what had been a temporary argument.

"Boot hill began filling up with the bodies of such men, and all too often, with the bodies of our own citizens, including our city officials.

"But then our esteemed marshal arrived and with his indomitable courage, his determination to administer the law to those would be lawless, and yes, through the swiftness of his gun, peace was finally brought to the town we call the Queen of the Border.

"Marshal Brown, we the citizens of Caldwell, owe you a great deal. And to honor your service to us, and to give you a visual token of our esteem, I now call upon Mayor Colson to make a presentation."

Mayor Colson had a very dark and well-trimmed beard. It was more than well-trimmed; it was actually cut in a pattern that circled around his jaw, but left open spaces in between the outer edge of his beard and the narrow spade of hair that dropped from his lower lip.

Mayor Colson picked up a beautiful .44-40

Winchester rifle. The stock was polished black walnut, the barrel was octagonal, and there was also a gold plate on the stock of the rifle.

"Allow me, sir, to read the inscription from the plate on this rifle," Mayor Colson said. He cleared his throat before he began to read.

"Presented to City Marshal H.N. Brown for valuable services rendered in behalf of the citizens of Caldwell Kansas. A.M. Colson, Mayor."

With a broad smile, Colson held the rifle out toward Henry.

"I'm overwhelmed," Henry said. "I don't know what to say."

"If I were you, Henry, I'd say thank you and take the rifle before the mayor gets tired of holding it out there, and changes his mind," Coop said.

Those gathered laughed at Coop's comment.

"Thank you," Henry said taking the Winchester.

The gathered businessmen and women applauded.

Henry grasped the rifle by the fore grip and held it up so everyone could see it.

"Thank you again," he said. "And I promise you this. I'll never give you cause to regret putting all your faith in me."

FOR THE LAST FEW MONTHS, it had become quite a common sight around Caldwell to see Henry Brown and Maude Levagood together at meals, or attending the theater, or even as an invited couple to social events sponsored by the school, the city, or some of the more affluent citizens of the city. Because of that, when Mayor Colson invited Henry to have dinner at his house that evening to celebrate the presentation of the specially engraved Winchester rifle, the invitation was extended to Maude as well.

Mayor Colson's house was one of the recently built two-story brick homes on Chisholm Street. It had a large wrap-around porch with bay windows on the ground floor and dormer windows sprouting from the roof.

The entry foyer had shining wood floors and a grand stair case that led to the second floor. A crystal chandelier provided light to welcome guests to the home.

Mrs. Colson met them, then showed them into the living room which with its elegant furnishings, carried out the theme of the house.

"Miss Levagood, I must tell you how much everyone in town appreciates all that you do for the children in our school," Mrs. Colson said. "Why it is said that the little ones just light up around you."

"I enjoy being around children" Maude said. "I think they know that, and when they realize that I like being with them, well, they just reciprocate in kind."

"Marshal Brown, you are a lucky young man to have such a lady as a special friend," Mrs. Colson said.

"Yes, ma'am, I'm well aware of that," Henry replied.

"Miss Levagood, did the marshal tell you of the presentation today?" Mayor Colson asked.

Maude laughed. "Are you kidding, Mayor? He won't stop talking about it. I'm pretty sure that by now he's shown that rifle to everyone in town."

The mayor nodded. "Good. We thought for a long time about how best to express our appreciation for the wonderful job he's been doing, and this is what we came up with."

"Mayor Colson, I can't think of anything I would have liked more," Henry said.

AFTER LEAVING THE COLSON DINNER, Henry and Maude were walking arm in arm on their way back to the hotel. It was only a block up from the mayor's house on Chisholm Street to the Southwestern Hotel.

"Mayor Colson has such a beautiful home, don't you think?" Maude asked.

"It's a nice house," Henry agreed.

"Oh, it's much more than a house, and much more than nice. It's a positively elegant home. Do you think we could ever have a home like that?"

Henry's heart skipped a beat. "We?"

"Henry Brown, I am not a one-night stand type of woman. We've been keeping company for a few months now, have we not? Perhaps it's time that you let me know what your intentions might be."

"Oh, Maude! Do you mean . . . are you saying that if I ask you to marry me, you would say yes?"

Maude smiled up at him, her eyes gleaming in the light of the gas lamp.

"Why don't you ask me and find out?"

"Would you marry me?"

"That depends," Maude answered.

"Depends on what?"

"Do you intend to give me my own home to live in, or do you expect me to move into your hotel room?"

Henry laughed. "I don't expect you to move into my hotel room."

"Then yes, Henry Brown, I will become your bride."

Henry started to kiss her.

"Henry, we're in public," Maude protested.

"I don't care if we're standing on the stage at the Opera House with a thousand people watching. I love you, Maude. And yes, someday we will have a house like the Colsons."

"Oh, Henry, is that a promise?"

"That's a promise."

"Coop, how about you having supper with me 'n Maude tonight?" Henry asked the next day. "On me," he added.

"I'd be glad to," Coop replied. "I'm not one to turn down a free meal, that's for sure."

Henry and Maude were already seated at a table when Coop stepped into the Medicine Lodge Café that evening. "I hope I'm not intruding," he said as he joined them.

"How can you be intruding when Henry invited you to join us tonight, Coop? Is it all right if I call you Coop?" Even though Coop had seen Maude many times, this was the first time she had ever called him Coop.

"Of course you may call me Coop. Everybody does."

"And you should call me Maude. Especially since you're Henry's closest friend, and the situation between Henry and me has changed."

"Oh?" Coop replied, with a puzzled expression on his face. "Changed how?"

Maude looked at Henry, and smiled sweetly. "I think I shall let Henry tell you the news."

"Coop, as you're my closest friend, I've convinced Maude to let me give you the news first." Henry reached across the table and took Maude's hand in his own.

"We are engaged. Maude and I are going to get married!"

"Henry, that's wonderful!"

"I knew you'd approve. I want you to be my best man."

"That's a task I'll be happy to perform," Coop said.

"It'll make ole Ben Wheeler a bit jealous that I'm choosing you over him, but you've been my friend a lot longer than he has."

"I'm honored that you asked me," Coop said. "When is the wedding to be?"

"I've already talked to Reverend Aikin. He allowed as he's never seen me at one of his church meetings, but he said he could marry us at ten o'clock in the morning."

"Ten o'clock in the morning? That's pretty quick, isn't it? You won't have time to invite anyone else to the wedding."

"There's only going to be four people there," Henry said, "Mayor and Mrs. Colson, you and Mrs. Rittenhouse, well actually, five counting the preacher."

"What about Ben?"

"Nah," Henry said with a smile, as he waved the comment away. "No sense lettin' him stew about you being my best man."

THE NEXT MORNING the wedding party gathered in front of Reverend Aikin, in the home of Mayor Colson.

"Marshal, I'll be happy to marry you and Miss Levagood," the minister said, "but first I'm goin' to ask you to take off your gun belt."

With a little chuckle, Henry took off his gun belt and handed it to Coop.

Less than ten minutes later, Henry Brown and Maude Levagood were married.

CHAPTER 23

A week after the wedding, Coop came into the marshal's office to ask a special favor of Henry.

"Sure, what is it?"

"There may be a newspaper for sale over in Medicine Lodge and I'd like to go see if that's true."

Henry chuckled. "Can't get the newspaper business out of your system, huh?"

"Well, you know what they say; some of us just have printer's ink for blood."

"Since you didn't sell the press you had in Tascosa, why don't you use it to start a paper here in Caldwell?"

"Believe me, when I say I've given that some thought. But there are already two papers in town, and there's not room for a third. Besides, Tell Watson has been a good friend to me, and I'd hate to go into competition with him."

"So what you want is a little time off?"

"Yes. Well, actually, it's more than that. I think I'd like to resign my position as deputy but I feel bad about that, because I don't particularly want to leave you in the lurch."

"In the lurch?"

"I don't want to abandon you, and leave you without a deputy."

"Don't worry about that," Henry said. "We both know Ben Wheeler's been after me for a job. If you really do want to quit, then I can hire him."

"In that case, the problem is solved for all three of us." Coop smiled, then he took off his badge and laid it on Henry's desk. "I'm now free to go start another newspaper, you have an opening and the salary to hire a new deputy, and Ben Wheeler will get his wish of becoming that deputy."

"I'm going to hate to lose you, Coop. Me 'n you've been friends for a long time."

"I'm not resigning from being your friend, Henry, just from being your deputy."

"Yeah," Henry said. "Yeah, that's right, ain't it? When do you plan on goin' to Medicine Lodge?"

"I thought I'd take tomorrow's train."

"All right, I'll tell the mayor, and then I'll put Ben on as my deputy today."

———

THAT EVENING, Coop joined Henry and Maude for dinner in the Southwestern Hotel.

"I'm sorry we have to host your going away party in the hotel dining room instead of our own house," Maude said. She looked pointedly at Henry. "But as you can see we don't have a house; we're still living in the hotel."

"I told you I'm going to build you a house and I will," Henry said. "These things take a little time."

Realizing that this was obviously a point of contention between the newlyweds, Coop felt a little uncomfortable and he said something to change the subject. "By the way, I saw Wheeler making the rounds."

"Yes, Ben was very glad to get the job," Henry said. "I'm goin' to miss you, you bein' over in Medicine Lodge 'n all."

"It's only seventy miles or so," Coop said. "Less than half a day by train. You and Maude will have to come visit me, once I'm settled in over there."

"We'll do it," Henry promised.

THE NEXT MORNING Coop took the train to Wellington, then changed trains to continue on to Medicine Lodge. The entire trip took about half a day, but had he gone by stage coach it would have been two days.

The largest building in town was the Grand Hotel, which somewhat resembled the Southwestern Hotel in Caldwell. Because he planned to spend at least one night in town, and maybe a few more, he walked across the street.

The lobby was large and pleasant looking, and there was a white-haired man occupying a chair next to a cold fireplace. The man was reading a book, but he was too far away for Coop to be able to see the title.

The desk clerk was making some sort of entry as Coop stepped up to the desk, setting his portmanteau on the floor beside him.

"Yes, sir?" the clerk asked, looking up from the tablet.

"A room please."

"And how long are you staying?"

"I'm not sure. I suppose that will depend on how my meeting with Mr. Payne goes."

"Ah yes, Mr. Payne. I'm sure that whether your meeting with him is for business or social, it will go well. Wylie has a way about him that makes everyone feel comfortable."

"It's my understanding that he owns a ranch with thousands of head of cattle as well as a mercantile, a bank, and a newspaper. Would you happen to know where would be the most likely place to find him?"

"Oh, he manages all his businesses from the bank," the clerk said.

"And where is the bank?"

"You can't miss it. Medicine Valley Bank is quite a handsome two storied, brick building. You'll find it on the corner of Main and First Street." The clerk chuckled. "It's literally on the corner, as the front door faces the corner itself, so the bank doesn't have a street address as such."

HALF AN HOUR LATER, wearing a clean shirt and vest, but without the deputy's badge on his vest, Coop stepped into the bank. There were two tellers behind the half wall and wire cage, and a customer stood in front. She was clutching the hand of a young boy. Sitting at a desk against the wall was a man in a suit. He appeared to be in his late forties or early fifties, and his brindled-gray hair was neatly combed. He also had a well-trimmed moustache, the gray of the moustache matching the gray of his hair, the combination giving him a very distinguished appearance. He didn't seem to be busy, so Coop felt no compunction about approaching him.

"Mr. Payne?"

"Yes, sir, how may I help you?"

"My name's James Cooper," Coop said extending his hand. "I understand that you might be interested in selling your newspaper."

"I may be," Payne said. "Are you interested in buying it, Mr. Cooper?"

"I may be."

Payne chuckled. "Well then, it looks as if we should have a conversation."

"I came over from Caldwell for that very purpose."

"What do you say we walk down and take a look at the operation?"

"That's what I want to see," Coop said.

"Mr. Geppert," Payne called out to the older of the two tellers. "I'll be out of the bank for a while."

"Very good, sir," Geppert replied.

"George is a good man," Payne said of his teller, as they walked from the bank to the newspaper office. "If I had had a person like George to manage the newspaper for me, perhaps *The Index* wouldn't be on the verge of bankruptcy now."

The newspaper was on Washington Street, a single story, wooden building with a large front window. A sign hung out over the boardwalk, and another sign was painted on the window, both saying the same thing: *Barber County Index*.

When they stepped inside Coop saw someone setting type, and he was surprised to see that the typesetter was a mere boy.

"This is Elmer Grant," Payne said, indicating the boy. "He's a hotshot type setter and press man even if he is fifteen years old. Elmer this is Mr. Cooper."

"Are you going to be the new editor?" Elmer asked. There was a hopeful sound in his voice.

"I expect we're going to negotiate that," Payne said.

At that moment a very pretty young woman came in through the front door.

"Papa, what are you doing here?"

Payne laughed. "I own the paper, Estella. Why shouldn't I be here?"

"It's just that . . ." Estella saw Coop, then stopped in mid-sentence. "Are you going to be the new editor?" she asked, duplicating Elmer's earlier question.

"What happened to your old editor?"

"Joe Johnson." Payne spoke the name with obvious rancor. "The scoundrel took three hundred and twenty dollars from the account in order to buy a new press. He got on the train and we haven't seen or heard from him since."

"That was six weeks ago," Estella said. "Elmer and I have tried to keep the paper going since then, but while I can write articles that might be of some interest to women, I haven't been able to do the type stories the men prefer."

"Plus which, the press is falling apart," Elmer said. "The frisket is loose and the tympan is so warped that you have to do two or three, sometimes as many as four impressions before you can get a sheet you can use."

"So you can see why I authorized Johnson to buy a new press," Payne said.

"What about this building, Mr. Payne?" Coop asked. "Do you own it?"

Payne nodded. "As a matter of fact, I do."

"If I were to buy the paper, would the building be included?"

"It wouldn't have to be if you don't want it."

"If I buy the paper, I want the building as well."

"Then by all means, we could make the building a part of the sale."

"Good. Could I look it over?"

"Certainly. You'll find Mr. Johnson's quarters in the back of the building. That is, they were his quarters, but they aren't now."

"If we would have checked earlier, we'd have known he had no intention of coming back," Estella said. "He took all his belongings with him."

"We didn't look because we considered those three rooms his private abode," Payne said.

"Where does the boy stay?" Coop asked.

"I live in the home," Elmer said.

"The home? What home?"

"The Baptist orphanage," Estella said. "Elmer has no parents."

"I'm sorry."

"That's all right," Elmer said. "I never have had any parents, at least none that I can remember. The people at the home gave me the name Elmer, and I don't even know what my real last name is, so when I was old enough to give myself one, I took Grant because of President Grant. I was left on the doorstep, like a puppy. "

Estella smiled, and put her arm around Elmer. "But it's like I told him, who doesn't love a puppy?"

Elmer blushed.

"As you can see, Mr. Cooper, if you decide to buy *The Index,* you'll have a built in staff, eager to go to work for you. But I'm afraid that your first capital outlay will be in buying a new press."

"I won't need a new press," Coop said.

"Mr. Cooper, you haven't seen this press yet," Elmer said. "I'm tellin' you, it's barely holdin' together."

"I won't need to buy one, because I already have one," Coop said. "I used to own a newspaper."

"What happened to it? Did you sell it?" Estella asked.

"No, the paper wasn't able to sustain itself."

"Mr. Cooper, if you couldn't make it with that newspaper, what makes you think you can make it with this one?" Estella asked, rather sharply.

"I don't know that I can," Coop admitted. He took in the newspaper office with a wave of his hand. "But it doesn't look like this one is doing all that well, either. Perhaps this would be a good time to give me, and the newspaper, a second chance."

Payne laughed. "I think he's got you there, darlin'. What do you say we give both Mr. Cooper and the paper, a second chance? Besides, if Mr. Cooper doesn't take over the newspaper I'll have no choice but to shut it down. That would leave you and Elmer without a job."

"You're right, papa. Mr. Cooper, I apologize," she said, contritely.

"No apology is needed," Coop said. He smiled broadly at the young woman. "And if you're going to work here, call me Coop."

THAT EVENING Coop was invited out to the Payne home for dinner. Elmer was invited as well.

"Wylie tells me that you're a city marshal in Caldwell," Mrs. Payne said from across the table.

"No ma'am," Coop said. "My friend, Henry Brown, is the city marshal and I was his deputy, but I resigned so I could come over here and buy *The Index*."

"Which he did," Estella said proudly. "And he's agreed to keep me on staff, which means I won't have to get a job in the Hog Lot Saloon as a percentage girl."

"Estella!" Mrs. Payne said sharply.

Payne laughed. "As you can see, Coop, my eldest daughter is full of vinegar."

Estella gave Coop a look that could only be described as flirtatious. Payne interrupted the look with his next question.

"You say the marshal is Henry Brown?" Payne said. "I've heard of him."

"What have you heard?" Coop asked.

"I've heard that he's very fast with a gun, and that he's been in many gunfights."

"He's been a law officer for nearly as long as I have known him," Coop said. In Coop's mind he was equating their time spent in the Regulators as being officers of the law. "So yes, I imagine he's been in a lot of gunfights. And yes, he is very fast."

"And you say he's your friend?" Estella asked.

"I think I'd have to say that he's my best friend."

Estella shook her head. "How can you be friends with such a violent man?"

"Sometimes a little violence is needed. Until Henry took over as the marshal, Caldwell was not considered a very safe town. It was too dangerous for anyone to walk the streets without the possibility of being hit by a stray bullet," Coop said. "Also, you may have heard how many law officers were killed in Caldwell, to say nothing of the mayor."

"Coop's right, Estella," Elmer said. "I've read all the stories about Caldwell that come in to *The Index*. And I've read how it's been cleaned up by the marshal." Elmer looked at Coop with an expression almost of awe. "You," he said. "Yes, I've read about you and how you saved a boy when the bank was being held up. You're as much a hero as Marshal Brown is."

Coop chuckled, self-consciously. "Hardly," he said. "It was Henry who prevented the robbery and saved the money for the town."

During the meal Coop talked about the *Tascosa Pioneer*.

"It was all I ever wanted," Coop said. "A newspaper in a growing town. I was sure we would grow together, but it wasn't to be."

"And so now you're about to jump back in the newspaper business," Payne said.

"Yes, sir, and I'm very much looking forward to it."

"When will you be bringing in your press?" Elmer asked.

"I'll be back just as soon as I can make arrangements to get it here," Coop said. "It'll be much easier to put it on the train, than it was when I brought it up from Tascosa."

"I have to say I'm surprised you hung on to it," Payne said. "I would've thought that when your newspaper went broke you would've sold the press."

"Believe me, I tried, but nobody wanted to give me more than half what I thought it was worth, so I just kept it. Maybe it was meant to be, because I always had it in mind that I wanted to get back into the newspaper business."

"You know, you're going to have your work cut out for you if this newspaper is to succeed," Payne said

"I know that's true," Coop said. "But, I'm starting out with one big advantage."

"Oh? And what might that be?"

Coop smiled at Estella and Elmer. "I've got an experienced and skilled staff, and they already know the town."

"We're going to make *The Index* the best paper in the entire state of Kansas," Elmer said with a wide smile. "I know we are."

"How can we lose?" Coop said, returning the boy's smile.

CHAPTER 24

Introducing Myself

I am James Cooper the new owner, publisher, and editor of the Barber County Index. My friends call me Coop and I hope, soon, to make friends of everyone in Medicine Lodge as I start my new enterprise here.

Although this paper and this city are new to me, the paper is not new to you. I am happy to say that I have maintained the same people who have been putting the paper out for you for some time now. And this dedicated staff continued to put that paper out even under the most trying of times.

Over the next several days I plan to meet and befriend, as many of you as I can. And I promise to give you a paper that will bring you the latest news of local interest, as well as news from across the state, the nation, and by the miracle of telegraph and cable, from around the world.

COOP MADE the daring decision to publish the paper every day except for weekends, and within two weeks he realized that his decision was going to pay off. His own stories had a sharp edge to them that the readers liked, and Estella was a very happy surprise to him. Her writing not only covered all the news of interest to the women in town, it did so with a wit and charm that had people cutting out her clippings to save them.

Elmer, in the meantime, quickly mastered Coop's Washington Hand Press, and because of that, Coop was able to augment the advertising revenue with income from special job printing.

One of the first things Coop did after getting settled in was to move Elmer from the home to the extra room in his quarters. It was mutually beneficial to both Coop and Elmer. For the first in his life, Elmer had his own room, and by living in the same building where he worked, Elmer was always available.

It was after the office was closed, but both Elmer and Coop were still working. Coop was writing advertising copy for the next day's issue, and Elmer was cleaning the press.

"You like her, don't you, Coop?" Elmer asked.

"I Like who? What are you talking about?"

Elmer laughed. "You know what I'm talking about. I'm talking about Estella. You like her, don't you?"

"Yes, I think she's a fine journalist."

"You know that's not what I'm talking about. I mean you *like* her."

"Well now, Elmer, I don't really see as how that's any of your business."

"Why, it is *too* my business. When you and Estella get married, I'll probably have to move out."

Coop laughed. "Whoa now, I must say, Elmer, you do move fast, don't you? A moment ago you had me liking Estella. Now you have me marrying her."

"Wouldn't you like to marry her some day?"

"I'd like to hear the answer to that question myself," Estella said.

"Estella! What are you doing here?" Coop asked, startled by her unexpected appearance.

"What do you mean, what am I doing here? I do work here, after all." Estella had a coquettish smile on her face.

SEVEN MILES EAST, in the dining room of the Southwestern Hotel, Henry and Maude were having their dinner. Maude was drumming her fingers on the table, indicating her irritation.

"Did you, or did you not promise me a house?" Maude said. "I'll answer the question for you. You did promise me a house. And yet here we are, still living in a hotel, having dinner, as we have all our meals, not in our own house, but in a hotel dining room. We have no privacy, Henry! We are a married couple and we are living our life in the public. Now you promised me a house, and I want it, now."

Henry smiled.

"What are you smiling about? It's not funny."

"We've got one," he said.

"What?"

"I bought us a house. I was going to surprise you with it when we moved in tomorrow."

"Oh, where is it? Is it on Chisholm?" Maude asked, excitedly.

"No, it's on Main Street, half a block north of Cherokee."

Maude's smile was replaced by a look of disappointment. "What kind of houses are on Main Street? Nothing like the fine homes on Chisholm, I'm sure."

"Just wait until you see it," Henry said. "I think you'll be quite pleased with it. I bought the lot next door to it as well, so we'll have plenty of room. And I bought a cow so we'll always have fresh milk."

Maude beamed, and reached out to take both of Henry's hands in her own. "I never doubted you, Henry. Not for a minute!"

"I DON'T KNOW," Henry said to Ben Wheeler a couple of days later. "I paid a hundred and sixty-five dollars down on the property which leaves me with a mortgage of seven hundred and thirty-five dollars. Then, to buy furniture, I had to borrow three hundred dollars from the Caldwell Savings Bank, and the only way I could do that was to have Levi Thrailkill and Bill Morris co-sign the note."

"That's a lot of money," Wheeler said.

"I know I'm in way over my head, that's for sure, but I had to do it. Maude insisted."

"Well, I'm not in as deep as you are," Wheeler said, "but I'm supposed to be paying support for my wife and kids, and if I don't come up with somethin' soon, she's goin' to wind up gettin' the law on me."

"Want some coffee?" Henry asked, starting toward the

stove where the coffee pot was.

"Yeah, thanks. Damn, Henry, you're in debt over a thousand dollars. Have you ever even had that much money before?" Wheeler asked.

Henry chuckled. "Yes, I have."

"What? How?"

Henry poured two cups. "Ben, if you ever repeat this to anyone, I'll deny it. But some years back I rode with Billy the Kid."

"Damn!" Wheeler said.

"We stole a bunch of horses and sold them, and my cut was nine hundred and twenty five dollars. If I still had that money my troubles would be over." Henry laughed, a short, self-deprecating laugh. "Too bad I don't know where to find another bunch of horses."

"I don't know where to find any horses we could get our hands on," Wheeler said. "But I know where we can find some money. A lot of money."

Henry frowned at Wheeler.

"What are you talking about, Ben?"

"Nothing. I'm not talking about nothin', Henry." He paused for a long moment, studying Henry's face. "That is, unless you're interested."

Henry didn't answer.

"So here's the question, do you want to get your hands on some money, and I mean a lot of money? Or do you want me to shut up about it and not say another word?"

"I might be interested," Henry said, cautiously.

Wheeler shook his head. "Huh, uh. You've got to be more than interested. If I say one word about it, you have to be all in. Otherwise, I don't say nothin'."

"Ben, if you have a way for us to make a lot of money, I'm all in."

"You know what I'm talking about won't be legal."

"I wouldn't expect it to be. Now, what do you have in mind?"

THE NEXT DAY Ben Wheeler brought two men into the marshal's office and introduced them to Henry. Both men were in their early twenties. Like Henry and Ben, both men wore moustaches and both were a few inches shorter than Ben's six foot. Their faces were bronzed, and there were sun lines around their eyes.

"This is Bill Smith and John Wesley," Ben said. "Both of 'em ride for the T5, and they're good, dependable men. They'll be just right for what we have in mind."

"Are you two men all right with doing what I say?" Henry asked.

"Yeah, hell, with the money Ben's talkin' about, I'm just fine with it," Smith said.

Henry looked at Ben. "The first thing I have to do is arrange with Mayor Colson for us to leave."

"Hell, what's there to arrange?" Wheeler asked. "We just go."

"Think about it, Ben. If we just disappear, people are going to start asking questions. But, if I have a reason for us to be gone, we'll have the job done and over with before anyone can even get suspicious."

"See there, boys," Wheeler said to Smith and Wesley. "That's why Marshal Brown is goin' to be in charge. He thinks about such things—things that me 'n you wouldn't even give a second thought to."

The mayor's office was in the same building, so Henry and Wheeler didn't have far to go to see him.

"Hello, Henry," Colson said, greeting his marshal with a broad smile. "What's on your mind?"

"Mayor, I just got word of a murderer who's hidin' out somewhere over in Barber County."

"Barber County? What does that have to do you? You're the marshal of Caldwell."

"That's true, Your Honor, but there's a twelve hundred dollar reward out for him, and I'd like you to give Ben and me permission to go after him."

"Oh, I don't know, Henry. With both of you gone, that'd leave Caldwell without any law at all."

"Look, Mayor, you know I just got married, and you also know that I just bought a house. That's left me strapped for funds and half of that twelve hundred dollars would really come in handy. I promise you, Mayor, we'll be back in a couple of days whether we find him or not."

Colson smiled, and nodded. "All right, you've certainly done a good enough job cleaning up the town that I'm sure we can get along without you for a few days. Also, I know you can use the money, so you and Deputy Wheeler have my permission to hunt for the murderer and seek the reward. What's the right thing for me to say, happy hunting? Or good luck?"

"I think good luck might be best," Henry replied.

IT TOOK HENRY, Ben Wheeler, and the other two men, less than half an hour to pack up and leave.

"You should 'a heard ole Henry spinnin' his yarn to the

mayor 'bout lookin' for a murderer," Wheeler said. "Damn, it was smoother 'n owl shit."

The other two men laughed as Wheeler recounted the meeting with the mayor.

Henry felt a sense of apprehension and an attack of conscience at what lay before them.

———

WHEN COOP AWAKENED in Medicine Lodge the next morning he was aware of three things: the sound of rain, the rumble of thunder, and the smell of brewing coffee. Surprised to be smelling coffee so early in the morning, he sat up, got dressed, and walked into the little kitchen that served the apartment. He saw Elmer sitting at the table with an obvious expression of nervousness. At that moment there was a loud peal of thunder, and Elmer flinched.

"Elmer, what are you doing up so early?"

"The . . . the thunder," Elmer replied.

"The thunder woke you? I guess it has been pretty loud."

"I'm afraid of thunder."

Coop chuckled. "Elmer, by the time you hear the thunder, the danger's already over."

"What do you mean?"

"The thunder comes after the lightning. If you're hit by a bolt of lightning, now that could kill you. But the thunder's nothing but a loud noise."

For just an instant the shadowed room was almost blindingly bright from a very close bolt of lightning, followed almost instantaneously by an exceptionally loud clap of thunder. Again, Elmer jumped.

"I don't care, I just don't like it."

"Look at the good side of it," Coop said. "It's going to start raining any minute and since we live right here in the newspaper office, neither one of us will have to walk through the rain to get to work."

"No, but Estella will."

"No she won't. Mr. Payne will bring her in his surrey with the isinglass windows. She'll be dry as toast when she gets here."

"Yeah, you're right. She will be, won't she?"

AN HOUR LATER, and two blocks away from the newspaper office, Wylie Payne sat in an overstuffed chair, reading the newspaper as he waited for his daughter to get ready.

"You know, Mindy, Coop is doing a much better job with this newspaper than Johnson ever did," Payne said to his wife. "I wish now I would've just hired him as my editor instead of selling him the paper."

"Oh, don't be foolish, Wylie," Mrs. Payne replied. "You have the ranch, the store, and the bank. You don't need that old newspaper. Besides," she added with a smile. "I have a feeling that soon, Mr. Cooper might be taking on a new responsibility."

"And what would that be?"

"Oh, for heaven's sake, are you blind?" Mindy nodded in the direction of Estella's room.

"Oh," he said. Then, in a more elevated tone. "Oh!"

"Papa, I'm ready to go now," Estella said as she came

into the room a moment later. She wrapped her arms about her and shivered. "Oh, I hate days like this."

"Don't worry, I have the surrey laced up good and tight. You won't get wet."

Estella shook her head. "It's not the rain, it's, I don't know, I just have a strong sense of foreboding."

"What you have, darlin', is a strong sense of imagination.

CHAPTER 25

HENRY BROWN, BEN WHEELER, BILL SMITH, AND JOHN Wesley had spent the night with a settler named Ben Harbaugh. Once when Harbaugh had been in Caldwell he had been braced by some drunken cowboys who wanted to have a little fun with the old man. Henry had come to his rescue.

"Mr. Harbaugh, I thank you for putting us up for the night," Henry said, "and, for this excellent breakfast."

"Well, it's like this, Marshal. Back when I was in the army at Ft. Riley, I was a cook. 'N the truth is, I miss it from time to time, so I was just real glad to be able to cook for you boys this morning. 'N after what you done for me when them men commenced to botherin' me, well, I figure I owe you."

"I expect them soldiers was some happy to eat like this," Wheeler said as he transferred another bite of pancake to his mouth.

"I do hope you boys find that murderer you're a' lookin' for," Harbaugh said. He laughed. "I'll say this for him, though. If he didn't have no place to get in out of the rain, well, he sure just spent him a wet night."

"That, he did," Henry agreed.

AT THE MEDICINE VALLEY BANK, Wylie Payne stood at the front window with his hands laced behind his back as he looked out at the rain. Water was running down First Street having made an odiferous slurry of mud and horse-droppings. Even the plank laid down at the corner to allow people to cross the street, was under water.

"Al, I hate to send you out in weather like this, but I need to get that packet of mail into the post," Payne said to the younger of his two tellers.

"Ahh, I'm not made out of sugar, Mr. Payne, I won't melt," Al Peacock said. The young man was in his early twenties and was apprenticing in the bank.

"I don't care what George says, I think you're a good man."

"What?" Al was surprised by Payne's comment.

When both Payne and George Geppert laughed, Al smiled self-consciously. "You were joking with me."

"The mail," Payne said, making a waving motion toward the door.

"Yes, sir, the mail."

Payne remained at the window for a few minutes after Al left.

"I doubt we'll get many customers this morning," Geppert said, "at least, not until this rain stops."

"I think you're right." Payne returned to his desk. "At least it's a good day to work on the account books."

IN THE OFFICE of *The Barber County Index*, Estella brought the article she was writing to Coop's desk for his approval.

Coop read the article, then laughed out loud. "Are you serious? There really is a family that has twins and one of them is named Amelia, and the other one is named The Other One?"

"They say they'll come up with a name later," Estella said, as she too was laughing.

"We'll run with it," Coop said. "Our readers will enjoy it."

AT THAT VERY MOMENT, Henry and the three men with him, approached Medicine Lodge from the west having circled the town.

"Damn, I wish this rain would stop," Ben complained.

"No," Henry said. "The rain's good. It's keeping people off the street."

"Yeah, I guess you're right."

They turned off First Street just short of the bank and headed for the coal shed which was just behind the bank.

"All right, Smith, you hold the horses for us while we tend to business," Henry said.

"Just think, Bill, next time you see us, you'll be lookin' at rich people," Wesley said with a big smile.

"Don't count the money 'till you've got it in hand," Henry said.

Henry, Wheeler, and Wesley sloshed through the mud. Henry and Wesley entered by the side entrance, and Wheeler walked around to come in through the front door. Wheeler started toward the teller's cage.

"It's a wet one today, I wasn't sure anyone . . ." Geppert started, but he stopped when he saw that what he thought was a customer, was holding a pistol in one hand, and a cloth bag in the other. Geppert threw up his hands.

While Wesley kept watch at the door, Henry, holding the Winchester that had been given him by the citizens of Caldwell, went to the empty cashier's window that was closest to Payne's desk.

Payne, seeing at once that it was a bank robbery, reached for a pistol. Henry responded by pulling the trigger on his rifle, then saw the sudden eruption of blood from the shoulder wound. The banker fell to the floor, groaning in pain.

Geppert rushed toward the open vault intending to shut the door.

"No you don't!" Wheeler shouted, shooting at the teller. He hit the teller twice, but even so Geppert was able to close the vault door and twirl the knob before he collapsed, dead.

"He shut the vault!" Smith shouted. Smith rushed to the vault door and tried to open it, but was unable to do so. "What'll we do now? The son of a bitch shut the damn vault door!"

Henry hurried to the front of the bank and looked out. The street that had been empty earlier, now had people who had been drawn by the sound of gunfire from the bank. One of those on the street was Sam Denn, the short, red-haired City Marshal.

"We've got to get out of here!" Henry shouted.

Henry stepped out the front door and began shooting. Although he didn't hit anyone, it did have the effect of clearing the street of people, including Marshal Denn.

The three men ran back to the coal shed where they found Wesley already mounted. Their horses were tied to a hitching rail.

"What did you tie them for? You were supposed to hold the reins!" Henry shouted as he, Wheeler and Smith struggled with the reins which, with the rain, were difficult to untie.

When finally they were mounted, they galloped down Main Street, the horses splashing mud and water.

THE SHOOTING COULD BE HEARD from inside the newspaper office, and curious, Coop stepped out to see what was going on. *The Index Office* was on Washington Street, half-way between Main and Spring, so as the riders galloped by on Main his vision was restricted both by distance and the rain, but he did get a pretty good look at one of the men.

And he could almost swear that it was Ben Wheeler.

But that was impossible! What would Ben Wheeler be doing here?

"The bank's been robbed! The bank's been robbed!" someone shouted, as he ran down Washington Street.

"Hold on there!" Coop called out to him. "What's going on?"

"The bank's been robbed. Geppert and Mr. Payne was both shot 'n Geppert was kilt."

"What?" Estella asked in a weak voice. "Papa has been shot?"

Until she spoke, Coop had been unaware that Estella was behind him. She started quickly toward the Main Street.

"Wait, Estella, I'm going with you," Coop called out to her.

There were several people already in the bank by the time Coop and Estella got there.

"They didn't get any of the money," Al said. "Mr. Payne said Mr. Geppert closed the vault door before they could get in. He closed the door even while he was dying. Who would have thought Mr. Geppert was that brave?"

"Where's my father? I want to see him!" Estella called.

"As soon as we can get a covered vehicle, we'll take him home. He was just shot in the shoulder, I think he'll be all right," Al Peacock said.

Estella and Coop hurried over to the wounded man who still lay on the floor. His head was elevated, because several had donated their jackets to make a pillow for him.

"Papa?" Estella sat beside him, and took his hand in hers.

"Coop?" Payne said. "It was your friend."

"What?"

"The bank robbers. The one who led them and the one who shot me was your friend, Marshal Brown."

"Then it *was* Ben Wheeler I saw," Coop said. He shook his head. "But why? Why would Henry do something like this?"

"Men, we're gettin' a posse up!" Barney O'Connor shouted. "Who's comin'?"

Coop reached down and, gently, squeezed Estella's shoulder. "I'm coming," he said.

Henry had arranged for fresh remounts to be posted in

the Gyp Hills in a place called The Gap. It was called The Gap because it was the only pass through Gyp Hills, although there were several blind canyons which gave the illusion of providing a way through.

Henry was counting on these blind gaps to confuse anyone who might be in pursuit. If the posse took the wrong canyon that would provide them with the time they would need to escape. And with the fresh remounts, they could easily avoid capture.

Those plans had been made when he was certain they would be fleeing the town with the money. Now they were fleeing for their lives, and had nothing to show for their misadventure this morning.

Henry knew the way to The Gap, because a farmer who was homesteading 160 acres had put up a barbed wire fence that pointed directly to it, and through which they would be able to get through the Gyp Hills.

What Henry and the others did not know was that, on the previous day, before the rain, the farmer had extended his fence by several yards and now it was pointing, not to The Gap, but to one of the blind canyons.

The four men rode into a steep, twisting gully, expecting to see fresh remounts just ahead. But after no more than a couple of hundred yards they realized they had made a big mistake and they saw, not their remounts, but fifty foot high walls ahead and to either side of them.

"What do we do now, Marshal?" Wesley asked. "The posse is right behind us, and we're caught in here like a rabbit in a trap."

"WE'VE GOT 'EM BOYS!" Barney O'Connor shouted, gleefully. "Them dumb sons of bitches rode right into Jackass Canyon 'n there ain't no way for 'em to get outta there 'ceptin' to come back the same way they went in. 'N we'll be a' waitin' for 'em."

O'Connor was right, the only way out was the way the four had gone in, and the posse saw the outlaws dashing back toward the opening. As soon as the two groups encountered one another, they began exchanging gunfire. The outlaws took shelter behind the rocks, just inside the canyon, and the posse did the same thing outside, keeping the outlaws trapped. The canyon rang with the sound of gunfire, but nobody was hurt.

"Hold your fire, hold your fire!" Coop called.

The shooting stopped.

"They can't go anywhere," Coop said. "They're going to run out of ammunition, food, and options soon. We can stay here a week if we need to."

"Yeah, the newspaper man's right," another of the posse said.

THE RAIN CONTINUED to fall and in the canyon the standing water got deeper and deeper. It was already nearly up to the outlaws' knees.

"Marshal, if we stay in here, this water's goin' to come gushin' in on us,

'n we're goin' to drown," John Wesley said. "I know, on account of I've seen it happen before, where dead end canyons like this fill up."

"John's right," Smith said. "We can't stay here."

"At this point, we don't have any choice in the matter," Henry said.

"Yeah, we do. I say we come chargin' outta here, shootin'," Smith said.

"There are four of us and at least ten of them," Wheeler said.

"That don't matter. Like the marshal said, we don't have no choice, 'n I'd rather go down shootin', than stay in here and drown."

"Quiet," Henry said. "Someone's shoutin' at us, 'n I know who it is."

"HENRY?" Coop shouted. "You know you've got nowhere to go."

"What the hell, Coop? Do you know them outlaws?" O'Connor asked.

"I know two of them," Coop replied without further explanation. "Henry?"

"Is that you, Coop?" Henry called back.

"What are you doing here, Henry? What in the hell took possession of you to make you try and rob a bank? And a bank in my town, no less."

"I made a mistake, Coop. A huge mistake."

"You sure as hell did. Now the question is, what are you going to do about it? You know we can wait you out."

"Coop, if we come out, can you promise me that we won't be lynched?"

"We're not looking to kill any of you," Coop said. "All we want to do is get you back to town and put you in jail."

"We're comin' out. Don't shoot."

"Don't shoot, hell," one of the posse members said. "I'm goin' to shoot the first one that comes out."

"You do that and I'll shoot you dead before the echo dies," Coop promised.

The four outlaws came out with their hands in the air. Coop walked over to Henry and stared at him with an expression that was a cross between anger and pain.

"It's funny, isn't it?" Henry said. "I mean, me bein' a lawman, windin' up in jail."

"There's nothing funny about this, Henry. Not a damn thing."

CHAPTER 26

THE RAIN HAD STOPPED BY THE TIME THE POSSE RETURNED to Medicine Lodge and because news of their arrival had gone before them, a crowd waited for them around the jail. There was a photographer there as well, and the four outlaws were shuffled into position to have their picture taken.

The last thing Henry wanted now was to have his picture taken, but he knew he had so say in the matter. Several of the town's people crowded into the picture as well. The way they were lined up Henry was standing between the two men he knew the least. John Wesley was to his right, and Bill Smith was to his left. Ben Wheeler stood to the other side of Smith.

As soon as the picture was taken the four were moved into the jail where they were allowed to change into dry clothes, and given paper and a fountain pen.

"What's this for?" Wheeler asked.

"This is in case you want to write to someone, to tell them where you are and how you wound up here," Marshal Denn said.

"Mister, I've got two wives," Wheeler said. "And I don't want to write to either one of them."

Henry heard the exchange between Wheeler and the jailer, and he saw that neither Smith nor Wesley chose to write. But he took the pen and paper.

Medicine Lodge, April 30, '84

Darling wife: - I am in jail here. Four of us tried to rob the bank here, and one man shot one of the men in the bank, and he is now in his home. I want you to come and see me as soon as you can. I will send you all of my things and you can sell them, but keep the Winchester. This is hard for me to write this letter but it was all for you, my sweet wife, and for the love I have for you. Do not go back on me, for if you do, it will kill me. Be true to me as long as you live, and come to see me if you think enough of me. My love is just the same as it always was. Oh, how I did hate to leave you on last Sunday eve, but I did not think this would happen. I thought we could take in the money and not have any trouble with it; but a man's fondest hopes are sometimes broken with trouble. I want you to send me some clothes. Sell all the things that you do not need. Have your picture taken and send it to me. Now, my dear wife, go and see Mr. Witzelben and Mr. Nyce, and get the money. If a mob does not kill us we will come out all right after a while. Maude, I did not shoot anyone, and did not want the others to kill anyone but they did, and that is all there is about it. Now, goodbye, my darling wife.

H.N. Brown

"YOU ASKED me to come see you?" Coop said, standing on the outside of the bars that were keeping Henry confined.

"Yes."

"I think I should tell you, Henry, that Mr. Payne just died."

"Oh," Henry said, closing his eyes. "Oh, but I shot him in the shoulder."

"The Doc said he lost too much blood and he died."

"That makes it murder. That's bad for me. That's very bad."

"That's bad for you? What about Estella? What about Mrs. Payne? What about Wylie's many friends? You took him away from all of us."

"I . . . I didn't mean it that way."

"What did you want with me, Henry, why did you ask me to come? Because I have to tell you I'm in no mood to do anything for you."

"I want you to deliver this letter to Maude. Will you at least do that?"

Coop was quiet for a moment, then he nodded. "Yes, I'll do that for you."

"Thanks, Coop. You're a good friend."

"No, Henry, I'm not your friend," Coop said. "Not anymore."

———

BY NIGHTFALL the crowds outside the jail had grown, and there were shouts of "Get a rope! Get a rope!"

Those shouts were answered by someone who said he had four ropes, he just needed four necks.

The town had only one pair of handcuffs and one pair of ankle shackles, so they made do by shackling Henry and Wesley at the ankle. Smith and Wheeler's wrists were manacled together. But Wesley discovered that the ankle shackle was around his boot, and he was able to pull his boot off. That left him and Henry free of each other.

It was a little more difficult between Wheeler and Smith, but because Smith had thick wrists and small hands, he was able to work the cuff off his wrist.

Outside the mob grew larger and louder.

"Turn 'em over to us!"

"No need for a trial!"

"We'll hang 'em tonight!"

"Boys, they're a' comin' for us tonight," Wheeler said, the tone of voice reflecting his great fear.

Henry felt the fear as well, and it ground away at his stomach, as if he had swallowed a badger that was eating him from inside.

The front door burst open and the mob rushed in. Henry lay coiled on the floor. Then, as soon as the cell door swung open, he got up and rushed through the crowd, managing to grab a pistol from the holster of one of the startled men.

COOP HAD COME down to the jail, not as a part of the lynching crowd, but as a newsman, an observer. He wished he could say that he was an impartial spectator, for that, the ability to step away from an event and observe it dispassionately, is what made someone a good journalist.

But he wasn't dispassionate. One of the men this lynch crowd was after was his friend, and regardless of what he had done, even though he had killed the father of the woman Coop loved, Henry Brown was still his friend.

"Stop 'em! Stop 'em! They're gettin' away!" someone shouted.

Shockingly, Coop saw someone emerging from the crowd, and even though the darkness was only partly pushed away by the light of a street lamp and a few burning torches, Coop could see that this was Henry Brown.

"Henry! Henry no, stop!" Coop called.

Henry raised his pistol and pointed it at Coop. "I'm not going to let them lynch me, Coop."

"Come with me, Henry. Let me hide you from this crowd; then, when it all calms down, you can go back to jail to stand trial." Coop started toward Henry.

"Don't come any closer, Coop. I don't want to shoot you, but I will."

"You don't want to do this, Henry." Coop continued walking toward his one-time friend.

"I warned you! I warned you!" Henry shouted and he pulled the trigger.

Coop felt the pop of air as the bullet whizzed by, and in a reflexive action he pulled his pistol and fired, hitting Henry in the middle of his chest.

As Henry went down, Coop holstered his pistol and hurried to Henry's crumpled form.

Astonishingly, Henry was smiling.

"Thanks," Henry said, his voice strained. "I knew I could count on you."

"You! You missed on purpose!"

"I didn't want to hang," Henry said. "I didn't want to hang."

Henry Brown's concern was justified, because within the hour the other three outlaws were taken to a grove of trees near Spring Creek and while nearly three hundred onlookers watched, the three men were hanged.

ONE WEEK LATER:

COOP WAS STANDING in the living room of the house Henry Brown had bought for Maude, having just given her Henry's letter, and the Winchester.

"What will you do now?" Coop asked.

Oddly, there were no tears in her eyes.

"I'm not sure," she replied in a voice that reflected no sense of loss or sorrow. "I only know that I will be leaving here."

As Coop took the train back home, he thought of the ten years he had known Henry, and of the strange way things had turned out. Surely there was a story here, and someday, someone would write it. He should write it. If anyone else did the story, they would paint Henry in only one shade, the shade of evil. And that was not the Henry Newton Brown, Coop wanted history to know.

Robert Vaughan sold his first book when he was 19. That was 57 years and nearly 500 books ago. He wrote the novelization for the miniseries *Andersonville*. Vaughan wrote, produced, and appeared in the History Channel documentary *Vietnam Homecoming*. His books have hit the NYT bestseller list seven times. He has won the Spur Award, the PORGIE Award (Best Paperback Original), the Western Fictioneers Lifetime Achievement Award, received the Readwest President's Award for Excellence in Western Fiction, is a member of the American Writers Hall of Fame and is a Pulitzer Prize nominee. Vaughn is also a retired army officer, helicopter pilot with three tours in Vietnam. And received the Distinguished Flying Cross, the Purple Heart, The Bronze Star with three oak leaf clusters, the Air Medal for valor with 35 oak leaf clusters, the Army Commendation Medal, the Meritorious Service Medal, and the Vietnamese Cross of Gallantry.

CPSIA information can be obtained
at www.ICGtesting.com
Printed in the USA
LVHW111815100119
603456LV00004B/588/P